Bull

© 2023 Susanne Bacon. All rights reserved.

No part of this book may be reproduced, stored in a retrieval system, or transmitted by any means without the written permission of the author.

ISBN: 9798370283925 (Print)

Cover photo by Susanne Bacon
Author photo: Donald A. Bacon

Because of the dynamic nature of the internet, any web addresses or links contained in this book may have changed since publication and may be no longer valid.

Susanne Bacon

Bulletproof

An Emma Wilde Novel

Other books by Susanne Bacon:

<u>*Wycliff Novels*</u>
Delicate Dreams
Wordless Wishes
Telling Truths
Clean Cuts
Haunted Homes
Suddenly Snow
Greener Grass
Major Musings

<u>*Other Fiction*</u>
Ashes to Ashes. An Emma Wilde Novel

Islands in the Storm

<u>*Non-Fiction*</u>
Home from Home

To Donald,

inspiration, husband, best friend

Preliminary Remark

The places, incidents, and characters in this novel are fictitious. Any similarities to actual persons, living or dead, as well as to any real events are totally coincidental.

Susanne Bacon

1

"… Of course, back in the day, we didn't make much of a fuss, and poachers were shot on the spot. A court case wouldn't have made sense, anyhow. Most of them were roaming the country without a permanent abode."

My head flew around to the speaker, a man in his late sixties who wore a three-piece suit with a watch chain and a silken neck-scarf. His lips were pursed, his thumbs stuck inside the pockets of his vest, and his eyes dared anybody of our guided tour group to protest such harsh measures. Ozzie nudged me as if to send me a signal that he knew I was about to question the justification of what seemed murder to me and that I'd be the only one to open my mouth. Meanwhile, the estate owner strutted up and down in front of us, droning on about the acreage of his property here and that of some place farther up north, near the Scottish border.

I let my eyes wander. We were standing in a great entrance hall designed to awe the visitor. It managed to impress me, indeed. So much history that was still part of the present. Anybody would probably become overly stuffy if they had their ancestral gallery staring at each and every movement they made. Not to talk of the coats of arms hanging on the walls in between their stern features and the knight's armors on both sides of every single door that went off the hall.

"… financing the lasting maintenance as an event location. Balmer Hall has been featured in several movies and has been popular as a photo location for weddings. But our main attraction are our hunting parties here and up north with balls and picknicks and all the traditions of what shapes a British hunting dynasty …"

I slipped my hand into Ozzie's as the group moved forward to a series of salons in green, blue, and gold, then to a dining hall. The eyecatcher here was obviously a paternoster that connected it with the kitchen below – kind of a wishing table version in the 19th century. The tour went on and on, upstairs, downstairs, down one hallway and up the next until we reached what the estate owner seemed to deem as the highlight, the armory. I saw Ozzie's eyes light up as he entered the room. Two long walls were filled with racks of what seemed to be almost identical rifles. A third side of the room was taken up by halberds, spears, and swords. But the fourth one was what drew Ozzie like a magnet.

While Sir Whatshisname praised the efficiency of the arms that the guests would receive on arrival to one of the hunts, Ozzie gazed at a display of historical guns and rifles that looked as if from the times of Sir Walter Scott.

"Check this out," Ozzie said half to himself. "A Winchester, a muzzle loader similar to mine back in the States, a US M1917 'Enfield', a James Bond gun, a …"

He lost me. I rather looked at the way his hyacinth-blue eyes sparkled, how his dark, short hair curled despite its military cut, how the muscles moved in his strong forearms that were bare even at this time of the year. I leaned into his side and gave him a hug. The group behind us was moving on.

"We should go along with them," I whispered. "Otherwise, we might get locked in."

"I wouldn't mind spending a night at the armory of Balmer Hall," Ozzie grinned.

"I'd prefer the carriage house," I countered and gently pulled him away from the display. "Come on, my whiz. I'd love to see one of these old closed barouches with curtains in the windows and ..."

Basically, if Ozzie had taken me to some huts in Timbuktu or to the Taj Mahal in India, I'd have been equally interested. But here I was in Suffolk, at a guided tour through a rural estate five miles away from the small and very picturesque village of Ealingham-on-Ouse, where Ozzie lived. The village, not the estate. It was my third visit with him, and I treasured each and every moment I shared with him anywhere more than if the Queen had presented me with a diamond tiara. At least, by now, everybody seemed to agree that we had something fairly unusual going between us. It had been different in the beginning, a bit over a half a year ago.

"You can't simply invite somebody you don't know at all to stay at your place! That is absolutely dangerous. What if ...?"

The suggestions as to what could happen to me were as colorful as they were obnoxious. All of them. People around me wrought their hands and shook their heads. They didn't even know Ozzie. In my late thirties and utterly self-reliant, I knew how to reason with myself and make my own decisions. Besides, it wasn't anybody's business but my own.

I prevailed. My invitation held. And nothing dangerous happened, at all. I simply fell hard for the person who this circus had been all about and whom I had come to know so well so fast. Oscar "Ozzie" Wilde, a U.S. Air Force Master Sergeant in his late thirties had popped into my life in a pretty dangerous situation. He had pretty much saved my life. At least, that was how I viewed it.

Actually, we had encountered each other for the first time at what would turn out to be a crime scene. Last May, we had both watched firemen trying to save an old barn with an attached home in my German hometown of Filderlingen, a suburb of the city of Stuttgart. Later that day, we had run into each other again at my favorite neighborhood pub. What had begun with some deep conversation and him traveling off on a mission very early the next day had turned into a series of phone calls during which he probably saved my life in calling the police about my investigation of another case of arson.

In fact, I hadn't realized that one of my colleagues at the newspaper for which I was working as a journalist was the arsonist. But he had been well aware that I was about to figure him out. My crime-reporting colleague Niko Katzakis and my friend

Linda, a police officer in Filderlingen, had managed to rescue me before that scum had been able to injure a horse and to damage even more stables. Or to kill me.

For my friend Linda the story had also ended in a love relationship. One that, for the first time, lasted more than a few weeks of insanity that amounted to the usual heartbreak of incompatibilities. This one culminated in an engagement. And I had gotten away with an egg-sized bruise on my temple – not the way I had intended to welcome Ozzie back for his first visit at my home, a few days later.

Anyhow, he had kindly overlooked my damaged face at the time and let it not hinder him from courting me in the most fulfilling way I could ever have imagined. I had fallen hook, line, and sinker for this guy. Thanks to cheap airfares between Stuttgart, the airport closest to Filderlingen, and Stansted, the one closest to Ozzie's home in Ealingham-on-Ouse, Suffolk, we had been able to visit and revisit a few times already. There had been a break of a month in between, filled with mutual yearning. That was when Ozzie had been deployed with a crew of other airplane maintainers to a place in Italy. But we still talked over the phone to each other, each and every night. It had become a daily ritual when we were separated.

When I had visited Ozzie for the first time, I had fallen in love with his home and lifestyle immediately, as well. Ozzie was stationed at RAF Mildenhall, an English air base that was mainly used by American forces. Mildenhall and Ealingham-on-Ouse, as any other settlement in the area, were surrounded by the Fens, an austere landscape consisting of diked pastureland and fields, crossed by countless drains, ditches, canals, brooks, locks, and small rivers. On the larger waterways, narrowboats traveled towards the seemingly endless horizon; or they were fastened to bollards on the banks, next to the towpaths. Lonely farmhouses dotted the pastureland, and church spires towered over cozy villages such as Ealingham. It was a wonderful scenery for walks and for letting your mind wander.

When I had announced my visit to Ozzie this time, he had told me that he would have to leave for a deployment to Morocco a few days into my vacation. I had been devastated and willing to postpone my trip. But Ozzie had asked me whether I could house-sit for him. Actually, he had made it sound so alluring that I simply hadn't been able to say no.

After landing in Stansted around five in the afternoon one dreary Thursday in November, I had jumped on the bus to Mildenhall, as usual. It was already dark outside, and the villages and small towns we passed by were but accumulations of lights in the distance. Nobody talked much; the silence was filled with the apprehension of reaching destinations. Newmarket was one of the bigger ones, and half of the people got off there. Soon, shop windows and pub signs swept by, again, and darkness enclosed us once more as we left the town on our journey farther north.

Just past Red Lodge, my cellphone rang. Ozzie's number.

"Darling," I whispered, so nobody on the bus would feel disturbed too much.

"Emma, sweetheart," his voice rasped gently into my ear. "You must be somewhere close to Barton Mills by now."

I looked outside the window and spotted the familiar neighborhood. "I am, indeed."

"Great. Listen, I'll pick you up at the bus terminal in Mildenhall, okay? So, don't call a cab in case I'm not there yet. I'm leaving the house just now."

"Okay. Oh, Ozzie, my whiz …"

Click. He had already hung up. I felt my heart beat higher, as I knew that he would meet me even sooner than expected. Has there ever been research about the relativity of the duration of minutes? Because this last quarter of an hour stretched even longer than the entire trip so far. At least, it seemed that way. But, of course, soon the bus took the last curves through the narrow roads of quaint Mildenhall and stopped next to the pavilion in the center of the terminus.

A long hug and some delicious cod and fries at *Mildenhall Fish & Chips* later, Ozzie and I drove past the long fences of RAF Mildenhall in his pick-up truck. The air base's floodlights lent the sky an orange quality where the runway supposedly was. Then, the deep darkness of the Fens surrounded us. Somewhere in the distance, I glimpsed the lantern tower of Ely Cathedral. In the marshlands on the other side of a small river whose name I didn't know, I spotted an open fire by a vague structure and smelled smoke in the air.

"Is anybody camping there this time of the year?" I asked.

"Travelers," Ozzie replied and threw a quick glance to the place I pointed out.

"Travelers?!"

"Or Roma."

I stared at Ozzie, who was looking straight forward, concentrating on traffic at a junction.

"Is there a difference?" I asked cautiously.

"The Travelers are of Irish roots. The Romany people are originally of Indian heritage. That's about all I know about their ethnicity. To be honest, I have never met any of them in person."

"I didn't know there were any here in Britain."

"There are. Some turned up in the Ealingham area about a month ago. Winter quarters, it seems. Most people don't like them. They distrust them. I recently drove past one of their sites, coincidentally. They stared at me as if I was a threat to them. And they had some big dogs running around, unleashed. I really felt uncomfortable. I have never driven down that road, ever since. I felt like I was intruding into a different kind of world."

"Hm. Maybe they *were* antsy because they encounter such distrust …"

"Maybe. I'm certainly not going back there and ask."

"If nobody ever cares about what makes them tick, how can we overcome such prejudices? Because I'm sure that's what they are. Prejudices."

"Don't even go there, sweetie. Don't forget, this is not your journalistic territory."

"True. But still some research …"

"Please …"

"Okay." I fell silent and stared into the dark where these mysterious people were carving out a life about which so little was known.

Then we entered Ealingham on its picturesque Main Street. Ozzie turned right into one of the first side streets and headed towards the Ouse dike. Ozzie's 70s' brick bungalow on a street running parallel to it didn't even have a number but sported the name *The Heron*. Probably because, at one time, one of these birds had dropped by on a regular basis. Being so close to the marshes and the river, it was a possibility. The front yard of the property consisted just of a towel-sized lawn and a parking spot for his Ford. The extensive backyard bordered on three other ones just as ample. So, though in walking distance to the center of the village, the entire place was quiet and secluded, especially outside the grilling season in late fall and winter when the other backyards were just as deserted.

When I entered Ozzie's home, I felt as if something inside me fell in place as soon as I stepped inside the door. Just as it had done the very first time. Maybe it was the home's unique fragrance. Ozzie claimed my nose was simply sensing mold. Everything in the Fens was in a constant state of humidity. Mildenhall even had the nickname "Moldy Hole". I just thought it was the smell of home – if there exists such an individual fragrance.

I happily settled in with my luggage. Some of my private items already had a permanent home in one of the closets and in Ozzie's bathroom. Meanwhile, Ozzie lit some logs in the fireplace, and soon we huddled in front of the flickering flames and let them toast our fronts. My mind drifted to the travelers in the marsh. Were they as happy and carefree as I felt at this very moment? I shuddered at the thought of how exposed to the outside world their fires had seemed. How vulnerable, compared to our cozy and sheltered homes!

We had the entire Friday and the weekend to ourselves and took walks in the area, some in Mildenhall along the river Lark, some on the towpath along the Ouse behind the dike in Ealingham. On Saturday night, after our return from that seemingly endless guided tour at Balmer Hall, we went out to *The Bird in the Bush*, a pub on Ealingham's Main Street with a beer garden in the back that on summer nights was full to overflow whereas in winter it was used by smokers only. The taproom was well occupied when we arrived, and Ozzie found us a tiny table next to an oak stanchion, close to the bar. Not a very private place with all the people piling up at the counter to shout their orders. But better than nothing.

It was the usual mix of weekend people. A few American military airmen, mostly keeping to themselves. A few older couples who would soon leave after an early dinner. And more and more young, local people pouring in to play pool or darts, and to get drunk. Ozzie and I checked the menu together, and after we had chosen our dinners, Ozzie went up to the bar and placed our orders, returning with a glass of beer for himself and one of cider for me.

"I wish the menus were what they used to be," Ozzie grumbled. "Ever since that big brewery bought this place and turned it into one of many, it's the same grub as everywhere."

"But they do have daily specials", I pointed out.

"Right. Probably the same as every single brewery pub of this chain. It's simply not the same as the mom-and-pop place it used to be."

"Well, things change over time. They might change back one day again."

"Hardly. Things usually change forward and rarely for the better."

"Are you in a mood tonight?!"

Ozzie gave me a lopsided smile. "Maybe. I hate to leave you and know that you will be alone in this village for the rest of your stay."

"I'll miss you, too," I choked. "But it is what it is, right? And there is fun stuff to do. There will be the market days. And on Wednesday nights there is Karaoke in here. And you are leaving your car here – so, that means my opportunities are almost endless."

At this point, one of the barmaids arrived at our table and set two well-filled plates in front of us. A moment later, Ozzie and I dedicated ourselves to our food. While I was chewing and enjoying my chicken curry with rice, I caught some commotion at the bar from the corner of my eye. I turned my head.

I spotted a young woman with slightly Mediterranean looks talk frantically to the publican, and then she handed him an envelope. She looked around as if haunted. For a moment our eyes locked. Then she turned, her colorful scarf which she was probably wearing against the cold outside slipping down her black glossy hair. One of the American guys at a table reached out for her, caught her scarf, and held it while he was saying something to her with a wide grin. She tore herself loose, scorn in her face, and rushed outside. The American guy got taunted by his chums, and for a moment their laughter drowned out the general noise in the room.

The publican, meanwhile, had taken the envelope, checked the room, and then gone to the telephone. He dialed, talked to somebody, and hung up. Then he placed the envelope by the phone and went back to work. Half an hour later – we had just finished our meal – an elegant young man of obviously upper-class circumstances strolled towards the bar, ordered a drink, and received that same envelope from the publican. He only took one sip from his glass. Then he left the pub.

"Did you see all this?" I asked Ozzie.

"See what?"

"The beautiful young woman who was accosted by the G.I. And the young man who just came in and left almost immediately."

"Maybe he was looking for somebody who wasn't here."

"Oh, but he ordered a beverage he didn't even drink. And he left with an envelope the young woman left at the bar earlier."

"Emma!" I heard in Ozzie's voice that his warning lights went on.

"Just saying," I soothed. "Looks like the publican is a dead whatchamacallit. Only that he is very much alive."

"The word is 'dead letter box'. But you're meaning a go-between."

"That's the word!"

"So, what if the publican simply did those young people a favor?"

"Yes, but the girl looked as if she were hiding from somebody. And the man looked around as if he were also on tenterhooks. And does this G.I. person grab at every woman or just at her because she seemed to be so different from anybody else in here?"

"I don't even know what woman you're talking about. As to my countryman – some simply behave silly when they've had a drink too many. And a lot of girls like their flirty ways." He wiggled his eyebrows.

"Great," I moaned. "It was plain boorish. And she seemed pretty annoyed about it, too. As if she didn't like him and just wanted to get out of here."

"Could it be that you are imagining something?"

"What if I have a hunch?"

"Emma, I don't like it when you're having hunches."

"Because they are usually right?"

"Because they usually get you in trouble."

"That's not fair."

"Please, just let it go."

After that, we talked about Ozzie's deployment. And I stowed my observations away for the time being. Time with the man I loved was too precious to waste on something that might be inconsequential, after all.

Ozzie started packing on Sunday night. I hated the thought of another farewell. That was the hardest part of our long-distance relationship. The constant extremes of exuberant reunions and heartbreaking partings. Adding the uncertainty when and where our next visit would take place, I sometimes wasn't sure whether my life was more often happy or unhappy. But I decided it must be on the happy side, as I couldn't imagine life without Ozzie anymore, either.

The next morning, we took leave at the front door. One of Ozzie's colleagues was already waiting for him in his car on the shoulder of the road. I was in tears, and Ozzie kissed me hard but tenderly. Then he took me by the shoulders, held me off gently, and looked me in the eye.

"I know that you love to take long walks. But I'm never sure whether it's safe for a woman to walk alone in the countryside. Promise me that you'll borrow my neighbor Henry's dog as a companion. I already talked to him about it. He's a bit hard to understand because of his dialect and some missing teeth. But he agreed. So, just go there, and ask him for Rocky. Promise?"

I nodded, in tears. Then I threw myself back at his chest for one more time before he had to peel me off.

"Gotta go now," he said hoarsely. "I'll see you soon again. Bye for now." He kissed me on the brow and walked over to the car that took him away from me.

I was left behind alone at Ozzie's home, a stranger in a small village in the middle of the Fens.

2

"Guess where I am!"

My friend Linda's voice was gushing through the receiver, and I had to hold it away from my ear because she was a little too loud for me this early in the morning.

"Why don't you just tell me?" I teased her back, dunking a teabag into my mug. I was only starting to enjoy my breakfast after I had slept in.

"Can you get yourself into a cab and come over to Newmarket?"

"You're where?!" I almost choked on a bite of toast.

The surprise call came only a couple of days after Ozzie's departure. It felt like a heaven-sent, as I had started feeling lonesome and a bit depressed. The house with its big kitchen, giant living and dining room, two big bedrooms, and the conservatory at the back felt eerily empty without Ozzie. Not that I wasn't used to being at his home alone. When I had been visiting him formerly, Ozzie had been working swing shifts on base more often than not. Which meant that I had had to see to my own entertainment all afternoon and early evening. But he was sort of around the corner and due to come back by the end of the day. Now, he was on a mission in Northern Africa, and I didn't expect to get more than a phone call from him every night.

I had taken up my daily walks with Rocky, a gorgeous black Labrador, all playful and curious. His owner, Henry Herbert, who was Ozzie's next-door neighbor, was a shy, elderly man with lots of gray hair and lots of missing teeth. After a few fruitless attempts to talk to me in his broad Suffolk accent, he had given up on my capability to understand him and just handed me Rocky, already on a leash. Otherwise, I had not much else to do than read, knit or embroider, and watch TV. Linda's sudden presence almost in the neighborhood, so to say, was more than welcome.

"I plan on having brunch or lunch at *The White Hart*," Linda told me. "I have been looking at horses at a couple of stables. Steffen wants me to choose one as a wedding gift for me."

"And Newmarket was the closest place you could think of?!"

"The closest to call on a certain, lately very elusive friend, too."

I laughed. "You are crazy!"

"It was Steffen's idea."

"Then *he* is. But tell him I love him for this idea of his."

"Will do. So, are you coming? I got to take the two o'clock bus back to Stansted."

Half an hour later I sat in a cab on my way to Newmarket. I was still wary of British left-hand traffic. Ozzie mastered it, but I had never even given it a try, and I wasn't going to do so in a hurry. I didn't want to risk damaging Ozzie's truck. Though I knew that sooner or later the day would come that I'd have to give it a go. Driving the truck, not damaging it.

The cabbie was a chatty guy who, as soon as he heard that I was German, began talking about his last trip there to watch a soccer game somewhere. While the landscape changed from the Fens to more and more agricultural surroundings and, then, paddocks holding horses, we talked soccer players and beer brand names as well as reminiscences of the last world championship. That is, *he* did. I just had to interject the occasional "M-hm" to keep my side of the conversation alive.

Finally, we reached the outskirts of Newmarket and drove down High Street to stop right in front of my meeting place with Linda. Squeezing myself out of the cab, I spotted her through the window of the hotel's restaurant and waved at her. A few moments later, I was inside and at her table. We hugged. She was beaming and looked more attractive than ever. Life as stable owner Steffen Mann's fiancée seemed to suit her very well. Her brunette hair was in a tidy ponytail, her curvy, long-limbed figure was dressed in a rustic blouse, jeans, and boots – a perfect fashion plate for a future stable-owner's wife. But above all, her eyes were shining with happiness, and her cheeks were slightly flushed. I almost felt dowdy in my non-descript jeans and cable-knit sweater, sandy mane all over the place.

"So, what's cooking?" she asked. "And did I manage to surprise you? And how is Ozzie?"

"One after the other," I laughed. Then I told her of Ozzie's deployment and how much her surprise visit meant to me.

"So, you have become your neighbor's dog walker?"

"Well, I guess it suits all three of us," I admitted. "It means that Mr. Herbert doesn't have to go outside in this nasty November weather. I enjoy the company of a living being that is utterly dedicated to making me laugh about its frolics and makes me stick to my daily routine of physical exercise. And Ozzie knows that I'm safe. That is, as safe as a dog's company makes you."

"Safe from what? You are living in the countryside, after all. It's supposed to be all quiet and peaceful."

"Don't you tell me," I sighed. "I think it's just a general feeling of unease around here, these days. Anyhow, Ozzie is always very protective of me. And he doesn't want me to run into any trouble."

Linda's eyes crinkled merrily. "Well, you and trouble *do* seem to have a special relationship, indeed."

"Oh, come on! Not fair. Just because of that one case …"

"Okay." She lifted her hands in defeat. "Anyhow, Ozzie doesn't strike me as somebody who is overly anxious."

I shrugged. "I agree. But then, I'm not sure what unsettling stories he might have heard. Anyhow, here I am walking the cutest, playful dog you could imagine."

Our food came – a full English breakfast for Linda, kipper for me – and we munched away, talking about Linda's horse viewing here in Newmarket. And then about her wedding that was to happen next spring.

"I imagine you to arrive in style. In a carriage with a coachman in livery," I joked.

"You know, I'm pretty sure that it will happen that way," Linda agreed. Then she went on about finding her bridal gown and about creating their wedding invitations. She sounded so blissful that I became a tad envious. I wished that Ozzie and I would talk similar future plans. But we saw each other too rarely. And though I felt that we complemented each other to perfection, I wasn't sure whether that was reason enough for Ozzie as well to consider marriage.

I was quite pensive when we left the restaurant after brunch.

"You have become quiet," Linda observed and eyed me sideways.

I shrugged. "Just a bit thoughtful," I admitted. "Not sure where Ozzie's and my relationship is headed."

"Well, then you should talk to him about it."

"Right. Great. But over the phone just wouldn't be right. And when we are together at these very rare and short occasions, time always seems to be too short for serious discussion. It's early days anyhow."

Linda made a non-committal sound. Then she headed to the windows of a bridal shop that we happened to pass that moment.

"Will you have a look at these?!" she exclaimed.

I gazed at a couple of dresses that couldn't have been more different from each other. One was only knee-length and very purist. The other looked like it came from a cotton sugar spinning machine, all frothy, flouncy, wide-skirted, glittery – a little girl's dream of what a princess might wear.

"Uhm," I just murmured. "We all know how tastes differ …"

Linda laughed. "True. I just wonder who would buy such a design."

"Very young girls with hearts full of romance and dreams of going to marry their fairytale prince," I ventured. "Let's go. I'm sure your dress will look totally different from any of these here. Tell me – is Steffen in on all your plans, or are you going to surprise him?"

While Linda was happily talking her wedding looks, catering plans, and the venue they had booked at Solitude Palace, a former hunting abode overlooking the city of Stuttgart, I just enjoyed having my now second-best friend with me while wondering what my best one was doing in Morocco, at this very moment. A country bus was roaring by, reminding me of Linda's limited time window in Newmarket. I sighed inwardly, torn between the happiness of now and the dreariness to return to in a few hours' time.

"Hey!" Linda's voice suddenly burst into my pensive bubble. "Look at this! What *is* this?!"

She pointed at a wooden wagon that was parked on a side street. Its roof was vaulted, its sides painted colorfully in the style of vintage circus posters. It advertised "Miss Lola's Palmistry, Crystal Ball Predictions, and Tarot". Next to the door at its back, there was also a price list. All in all, it looked like a thing of a past long ago.

"Roma, I guess," I muttered.

"What? I didn't know there were any in Britain."

"Me neither until very recently. Some have their winter quarters close by Ealingham. Fortune telling is one of their traditional income sources, I guess."

"Oh my! This is too much fun. I want to try this. Can we try this? Please? I want to know how close to the truth they can get."

"Uhm, not very keen on fortune telling," I refused.

"Oh, come on! It won't hurt!"

"Won't do much good, either," I retorted. "Maybe I prefer surprises."

"I want to go. Definitely."

Linda tried to stare me down. She looked like a little girl who wanted to get her way desperately. I had to laugh.

"Well, you go ahead. I'll wait outside." I pointed to a bench on High Street. "Take all the time you need. And take the predictions with a grain of salt."

Linda grinned. "Oh, it's merely a game to me. No worries."

I watched her turn around and head for the wagon. She hesitated a little before she set her foot on the lowest step. Maybe she had the jitters, after all? Then she knocked on the turquoise door with its red lettering and gilded ornaments. A moment later, the door was opened, and a middle-aged woman in Romany costume appeared in the opening. I stood too far away to hear what words they exchanged. But I saw the Roma lift her face for a moment as if she had sensed me watching her. She said something to Linda, who turned her head and made a dismissive gesture. I felt a bit embarrassed to have gawked so openly and walked off to the bench I had indicated to Linda. I sat but couldn't help looking back one more time, only to see the wagon door close on Linda and the Romany woman.

I shuddered slightly. I had never been superstitious, but I also believed in things between heaven and earth that we can't fathom. Was it that I was scared that somebody might have insight into my future for whatever reason? Was I scared more of their knowledge or of what might lie in wait for me? What made me feel so wary about a Roma in a cliché costume with a cliché occupation in a cliché little wagon?

I sat there, pondering. I didn't pay attention to what was going on around me or who was passing by. I didn't even check my watch. But I was almost startled to death when a smooth English voice spoke up right next to me.

"Before you travel to another world for good, beware of bullets!"

My head flew around, and I stared right into the eyes of the Romany woman. She was strangely beautiful in a slightly wilting way, her dark green eyes boring themselves into mine, her mien bewilderingly intense. Her bangles were clinking as she made the sign of a cross above my head as in a blessing. Then she turned, her wide, long skirt whipping around her bare ankles, the tassels of her colorful shoulder scarf flying.

"What?"

But she didn't repeat her words. She walked to her wagon and disappeared behind the turquoise door. Linda stood at the foot of the wooden steps, looking dazed. I slowly rose and approached her.

"What was *that*?! Did you just hear this?"

Linda shook her head as if waking from a dream. "I can't believe what things she knew about me."

I realized that my friend had been too occupied with her own experience to have paid any attention to what had been going on between the Roma and me.

"How was it?" I asked.

"She knew just everything. That I'm a policewoman, that I'm here to get my wedding gift. That my wedding will be in spring. She knew about the bad luck I had with love till recently. She said that my path would be long and straight but not always easy."

"Yeah," I mocked. "That probably goes for any law-abiding citizen."

Linda lost her dreamy gaze now and looked at me, almost outraged. "You shouldn't take this so very lightly. There was a lot of truth in what she said."

"Which apparently was little enough. I hope it didn't cost you an arm and a leg."

"She asked whether you were my friend even before we entered her wagon."

"Well, that was an easy guess, wasn't it? She probably saw us discuss your visit with her before you knocked on her door."

"Well, she said she had a special message for you."

"I hope she didn't make you pay for that, too."

"No, she didn't. But, come to think of it – she was a little absent-minded at first and only got it together after I crossed her palm with silver. And after she was finished telling me my fortune, she just got up and left. Did she say anything to you?"

"Nothing important," I evaded.

But for the rest of Linda's visit with me, my thoughts kept returning to the strange warning the Roma had uttered and to its implications. When I returned to the wagon after having seen off Linda on her bus to the airport, the turquoise door was secured with a padlock, and the price list next to it was gone. The vehicle was deserted. I wasn't sure whether I had hoped to encounter the fortune teller again to ask her anew what she had meant with her words. Or whether I was glad she wasn't available for business anymore because, now, I could simply discard her strange message.

3

Rocky was running far ahead of me as he usually did on our walks along the river Ouse once I clipped him off the leash. But on this slightly drizzly gray afternoon a day after Linda's visit in Newmarket, this playful black Labrador seemed even more inquisitive than ever. He stopped at seemingly every bench and pollard on the towpath, sniffed it, circled it, rushed back towards me, and ran off again. It was as if he had a crazy amount of extra energy on top of his usual high level of it. I just didn't feel it today. I huddled into my coat and scarf, pulled my woolen hat a bit lower into my brow, and blew into my cold hands, as I had forgotten to bring my gloves along.

As usual, this afternoon I had walked away from Ozzie's red brick bungalow on the fringe of the village, picked up Rocky next door, passed through the floodgate in the dike with him, and turned into the towpath by the river Ouse. We had been there only for a few minutes, and I was pondering what to do after the walk when my train of thoughts was suddenly interrupted by the sharp sound of a shot. I looked around but couldn't see anybody. I knew it was the hunting season. But a shot this close to the village was something rather unusual. Especially a single one. Usually, you knew a hunt was going on when there were several shots and they sounded from one of the estates farther away. So, chances were that this wasn't a hunt, at all. But then, maybe, it hadn't been a shot, either. Just a sound like one.

Rocky, who was way ahead of me, had stopped abruptly, too, and looked back at me. Had he also been startled? But maybe I only imagined it. The river and, accordingly, the towpath bent out of sight behind the dike. Rocky stood there, wagging, and probably wanted to make sure that I was still following him before he went on.

"It's okay," I called out to him. Then I muttered to myself, "Probably just a car engine's backfire."

Sure enough, a few moments later I heard the deep rumble of a vehicle moving past on the other side of the dike. Rocky trotted on and disappeared behind the bend. I, too, continued my walk, gazing at the slow, murky water of the river and the grayish-yellow marshes on the other side. I was lost in my thoughts when Rocky rushed back at me with a bloody nose, yelping and whining.

"Oh my gosh, Rocky!" I cried out. "Are you hurt?"

He jumped at me, then frantically ran in circles around me. He totally spooked me with his peculiar behavior and his gory face. I bent down and managed to catch hold of his collar to get a closer look at him. But there was no wound on his nose. And his mouth didn't show signs of blood, either.

"Where did you bloody yourself, boy? Did you find and kill a rabbit?" I asked myself more than him, of course, while putting him on his leash again. "Is that what has made you so excited? Is it your natural hunting instincts?!"

I sauntered on with him but, at one point, Rocky refused to go on and simply plopped down on his haunches. I tugged at the leash, but he wouldn't budge. Instead, he whined again, stared at a spot in the high grasses on the river bank, and barked.

Now, Rocky wasn't a barker by nature. And that made me suspicious. I followed his gaze and then gasped. I started to tremble. Was this the sole of a shoe that I glimpsed between the dense, high blades?

As fast as I could, I wound Rocky's leash around one of the bollards close by. Then, I walked towards that spot. As soon as I reached it, I gagged. For it was not just a shoe. A young man's body was attached to it, lying in the grass, very limp and lifeless. He wore blue jeans and a woolen jacket checkered in gray nuances; a matching gray shawl was loosely tied around his neck. The scarf his right hand was clutching stood out all the more with its bold colors and folkloric pattern. A single streak of blood ran across the tan face from a distinct hole in the brow and vanished in his tousled black hair. Beyond the head was an indescribable mass of which I didn't even want to know what it was. I gagged more violently and stepped backwards, almost stumbling over another bollard.

I turned around and ran towards Rocky, who was barking again and tore at his leash. For whatever reason I felt safer when I had reached him. I sat down on the cracked wet asphalt of the towpath. I heard somebody sob dryly "Oh my God, oh my God" again and again until I realized, after a while, that it was myself.

Only then did I start fumbling for my cellphone in my coat pocket. The silk lining seemed to hug it intimately while my attempts to wrest it from it ended in a rip of the material. Flip it open. What was the emergency number in England? Oh my, what …? 999, my trembling fingers dialed. After a single ring, my call was answered. I was shaking so badly by now that I almost dropped my phone.

"Hi, I think I just found a corpse," I hyperventilated. Then I took a deep breath. I knew better than to blurt out what came to my mind first. "This is Emma Schwarz. Yes, it's a German last name." I started spelling it out, then described where I had found the body. Later, I wouldn't even remember what else I said to the dispatcher who was cool as a cucumber, then told me to stay right where I was and not to disturb the site. They'd be sending somebody immediately. Then he hung up. I bent over and started to dry-heave. A few minutes later, I heard sirens approach from the village of Ealingham.

Shortly afterwards, voices came closer beyond the bend and, then, two policemen strode towards me very fast.

"Are you Emma Swart, the person who called in the body?" one asked. He was wiry and very young, probably as shortly out of police academy or what they called it over here as the other one seemed close to retirement.

"Schwarz," I corrected him. "Yes." Then I pointed towards the place where the body lay. "He's over there." I pressed my fist against my mouth, trying to fight down another wave of nausea.

"Are you okay?" his older, slightly shorter, and broad-shouldered colleague asked me. "Sergeant Cameron, by the way. And that is Constable Williams."

I shook my head, then nodded. "Kind of," I replied. "At least, I'm not the one who has been shot."

Meanwhile, Constable Williams had walked over to the body, taken a look at him, and turned around with an ashen face. He probably wasn't used to such sights in this otherwise pastoral scenery, either. He grabbed a radio from his hip holster and started talking into it. Then he returned to us.

"Crime scene tape", he announced shortly and visibly shaken.

"Bring a space blanket from the car as well," Sergeant Cameron said as he looked at Rocky. "So, *he* found the body? Did he move him any?"

"I don't know. He came back with his nose all bloody. So, he obviously must have sniffed him out."

"Did *you* touch the body or move it?"

"Heavens, no! I just looked at him from where you can see his shoe. He was shot in the head. The sight of that almost made me throw up." I gagged again. "I think I even witnessed the shot. I mean, the sound of it. But I thought it was a backfiring car engine."

Sergeant Cameron swayed his head pensively. "So, you didn't see the shooter?"

I negated.

"And that shot – when did you hear it?"

"Ten minutes ago? Fifteen minutes ago?" Why hadn't I looked at my watch? Because I had heard the car shortly afterwards and, therefore, drawn a wrong conclusion.

Sergeant Cameron took down a note. I hadn't even observed that he had taken out a notepad and ballpen. I started to shiver.

"Have you ever seen the victim before? When he was alive yet?"

"I wouldn't know. I'm not sure. I think, no." Why was I so bewildered? Because something about the victim had struck me, though I didn't know the man. I just couldn't come up with what it was.

Sergeant Cameron nodded. "Well, be ready to be asked more questions later."

"But ..."

"I know, right now, you are in shock. But later, you might come up with more details. And the CID will definitely want to talk to you, too."

"The CID?"

"Stands for Criminal Investigation Department."

"Oh. Okay." I rubbed my arms to get rid of the shivers that went up and down my entire body by now.

The next few minutes were spent with me telling Sergeant Cameron my contact information here in Ealingham and over in Filderlingen. Then, Constable Williams reappeared with a roll of crime site tape in one hand and a space blanket in the other. He handed Sergeant Cameron the golden foil and returned to the crime site with the tape. Sergeant Cameron gently laid the blanket over my shoulders. Then he took a small metal flask out of one of his breast pockets. He offered it to me.

"Haven't drunk from it yet. But it might soothe you. It's a fine Scotch." Then he frowned. "You haven't come here by car, have you?"

I smiled weakly. "No, Sergeant. But I'm not into drinking this time of day, either."

"Just a sip," he commanded. "It will make you warm and take off the edge."

I obeyed and lifted the flask to my lips. The liquid burned my mouth, and the bittersweet flavor of peaty whisky hugged my tastebuds. As I swallowed, the heat ran down my throat and slowly settled in my tummy from where its rays reached out to my skin.

"Now another one," Sergeant Cameron said. "You can't stand on just one leg." He winked.

The second sip did its job. I handed the flask back to the policeman and pulled the foil closer around myself. He screwed his flask close and placed it back in his breast pocket, looking satisfied.

Now I heard more voices approach where the two of us were on the towpath. I turned around and saw a number of people, some in police uniform, some in plain clothes, walking purposefully towards us.

"Will you and your dog be able to go home from here?" Sergeant Cameron asked me quietly. "Or do you need a ride?" He patted Rocky, who in turn began to sniff him out and lick his hand. "Because you cannot stay down here any longer. This is a crime scene now, and we'll tape it off altogether until further notice … Which means that this path will be closed in either direction."

"I'll be fine," I said, starting to feel a bit better although the past quarter hour – was it that already?! – seemed so utterly surreal. I took off the space blanket and held it out to him.

"Nah," Sergeant Cameron declined. "Keep it around yourself until you are thoroughly warm again. Can't be reused on anybody else anyhow."

"Thank you," I said, but his attention was already with his team, and I felt dismissed. As the newcomers identified their names and ranks to the sergeant or were greeted as old acquaintances, I quietly untied Rocky's leash from the bollard. He looked at me with bewildered dog eyes, then rose, and pressed himself tightly against my legs.

"It's okay, buddy," I assured him. "Everything gets taken care of now. We can walk home."

But after hiking back on the towpath and passing through the floodgate, I pensively looked back once more. Of course, the bend in the path hid the crime site now. So, there was nothing to see but the river and the seemingly calm landscape in which not an hour ago a young life had been brutally extinguished.

I had never seen a gun wound before. Only the stuff that movie studios create. I couldn't remember whether a gunshot to the head always blew out matter. What I had seen had been sickening. And somehow, I felt violated by the shooter as well. He or she hadn't taken in account that an innocent bystander would discover the body. That my peace of mind would be disturbed. Not just because of the gory find in itself. But even more so because of the question, why. I was a journalist, after all. And though not specialized on crime stories and judicial reports, a journalist pretty much thinks along the same lines as a detective. A story well researched has to answer at least five aspects: who, when, where, what, and why. This murder victim was part of a story. And though the sight had sickened me, I also felt curiosity stir in me. Who had done this? And why?

"Come on, let's find out something," I encouraged Rocky, who was sniffing a post of the floodgate now. He wasn't aware that I went back in the direction from which we had just come, only on the village side of the dike. We passed police cars and an ambulance that were parked on the road shoulder. I checked where the dike made its slight bend. Then I started climbing it while Rocky was keenly tearing ahead on the leash. On top of the dike, he simply sat and looked at me, panting, as I stopped by his side.

Yes, this was the right spot. I was aware that I shouldn't be up here because this might be considered part of the crime scene, as well. It just hadn't been taped off yet. Below, I could discern the taped-off section of the towpath. Somebody took photos, another person measured items, distances, whatever. I tried to avoid looking at those parts of the body that were not hidden by the people who were working the scene. Would the distance have been close enough for killing a person with a pistol or a revolver? Or had they used a rifle?

I checked the angle in which the body was positioned to the dike. I walked on until I was in a straight line with the feet. This must have been the spot where the shooter had taken aim. About a hundred yards away.

"Why did I know that you would come here?" Sergeant Cameron's voice startled me out of my thoughts. He had come up from behind and was looking stern now. Not like the almost grandfatherly man he had been before. "You know that you are possibly destroying clues?"

I blushed. "I'm sorry," I blurted. "It only occurred to me just now. I simply can't wrap my head around it that I heard the shot. And that shortly after ..." I bit my lips.

"Well." He seemed to mellow a bit now. "I understand that it will occupy your mind for a while yet. But you better return home now and leave things to the police."

I nodded and turned my eyes to the ground to find safe footing for the descent. A sudden movement from Rocky's end of the leash made me look up again, and in this fracture of a second, my eyes caught a faint gleam. Something metal.

"There!" I called out and pointed to a tuft of grass right behind the sergeant.

"What?!" he asked. "Trying to distract me?"

"No, Sir! Right behind your left foot. Is that …?" I left the question hanging in the air.

Sergeant Cameron carefully stepped forward, then turned around in the attempt not to step onto what I thought I'd discovered. He whistled through his teeth, reached into his breast pocket – not the one with the flask – and pulled out a marker and the equivalent of a Ziplock bag. He bent over, stuck the marker into the ground, and placed what I had pointed out into the plastic bag without touching it. Then he straightened up and looked at me with an almost mischievous grin.

"You know, I should punish you for your intrusion and not even show you what I just bagged." I felt my face fall. "But I'm not a mean person." He held out the Ziplock bag to me. "It is a cartridge case."

I glanced at the brass item. "It's huge! What kind of a pistol shoots this?!"

"Rifle, rather," he said dryly. He looked at it closer himself now. "Centerfire. Large caliber. 30-06." He looked at me and squinted his eyes. "I don't know why I'm telling you this. My gut tells me you are a meddler."

I swallowed hard and smiled sweetly. "It's normally my job. I told you I'm a journalist."

"Well, but you are not working over here. We don't even know whether the case belongs to the bullet that killed the poor lad. So, you better call it a day, and end of story."

He sounded stern again. He might have had some run-ins with journalists back in the day, I thought. Also, I knew that soon his own territory was going to be invaded by total strangers from a department specialized in murder. He would be handed the credit to have secured the crime site. That would be *it*. The honor of discovering the killer's identity – if ever there was such a chance – wouldn't be his but somebody's from a place higher up, farther away.

I felt sorry for him. He seemed to be a kind guy, after all. Somebody who probably played with his grandchildren when he had a weekend off. Somebody who was chummy with everybody who counted in Ealingham. I had better stay on his good side. Especially, since I was only a guest in this country – just like the guy at whose home I was currently staying.

"Heard and understood," I muttered demurely. "And sorry, again."

"It's for your own good, kid," he replied and suddenly looked worried. "You don't want to get involved where a killer has wreaked havoc. Leave it to the pros, okay?"

I nodded.

"I mean it."

"I hear you."

"I don't want to see you up here again in the coming days."

"You won't," I said.

I didn't know that I'd break my promise within less than twenty-four hours.

4

I dropped off Rocky and left Henry, just muttering my thanks for letting me walk his doggie. I never mentioned to him what part Rocky had played in this afternoon's horrific discovery. Nor about the latter, at all. Then I unlocked the front door to *The Heron*. The slightly musty air struck my nostrils but didn't bring me its usual comfort. I closed the door behind me, leaned against the wall next to it, and closed my eyes for a moment. Then, I slowly peeled myself out of my coat and hat and hung them on the wall rack.

The house was quiet. I only heard the old grandfather clock tick in the living room. And then, Rocky's happy bark from the backyard next door. I sighed. Solitude was not what I wanted right now. Not with the kind of situation from which I had just walked away. If only Ozzie were here. If only he came back from base tonight.

Ozzie ... Just thinking of his name made me yearn for his sonorous voice, his hyacinth-blue eyes. To dig my hands into his short black curls. To tell him what had happened this afternoon. Though I knew it would bother him, big time. He had already been worried that I might encounter whatever crime was lying in wait in the area during his absence. And indeed, I had. This hunch had been *his*, and he hated hunches in general.

I paced the kitchen. It was one of my favorite rooms in the house: lots of workspace, walking space, and a big window that overlooked the backyard. Dusk started setting in early these days, and the trees and bushes outside turned into darker blotches against a monotonously dark-gray evening sky. The potted herbs Ozzie kept on the window sill looked cheerfully green and gave off a mild, savory scent. The fridge was humming, and the heater kicked in, as the house was slowly cooling off. It could have been so cozy inside, but I felt shiver after shiver run down my back. Probably the after-effects of the shock.

Finally, I decided to brew a cup of Lady Grey tea just in order to keep me busy. Maybe, it would make me feel warmer, too. I rummaged through one of the cupboards and found some half-stale scones that would go with it. I didn't feel hungry. I just wanted to do *something*.

As the electric kettle increased its noise and I grabbed one of Ozzie's numerous mugs from one of his many deployment locations, I went over the facts I had been able to gather this afternoon. Not that there had been that many. But getting one's ducks in a row was key in telling a story as a journalist. Or in detecting the reason why an event had happened.

The kettle clicked, and I poured the boiling water over the teabag in the mug. I inhaled the fragrant steam and bit into one of the scones. Ugh – Ozzie should have tossed those. They had lost their light texture, and the staleness didn't really add to the experience of eating them.

Swallowing the mushy goo, I returned to my train of thoughts. So, I presumably had heard the shot that killed the young man in the Ouse Fens. And shortly after, a car had driven past behind the dike. From the sound of it, it had been a big SUV. Maybe, the vehicle and the shot were connected. But so far, this was only conjecture. The young man might have been shot earlier, and the sound I had heard *could* have been the SUV's backfire. On the other hand, I had never heard a second shot-like sound earlier, which would have been the case had there been a shooter *and* that car noise, as I was living close enough. Which ruled out that the sound's cause had been the SUV.

The young man had lain face-up in the slough grass. That meant he must have looked his killer in the eye. That, again, could mean three different things. Maybe, he had known his killer and, therefore, looked at him. Maybe he had just coincidentally looked into the direction of the dike. Or he had been called to look at the shooter, then been shot.

Something about him had also looked vaguely familiar, although I was absolutely certain that I had never before encountered him. I was not sure what it was. What also had struck me was his swarthy skin. Wait! Could he belong with the Romany people who lately roamed the area? Had he lived at one of their winter quarters? I'd have to check on that.

Then, I thought of the caliber of the ammunition. Sergeant Cameron had shown me the empty case and mentioned that it was a large caliber. Well, I wasn't familiar with any ammunition, to be honest. But that the case was large had been obvious even to somebody as unknowledgeable of weapons as me.

I checked the kitchen clock. Four minutes had passed. I removed the tea sachet from the mug and dumped it into the sink. Then I grabbed the mug and the scone and walked over into the dusky living room where I dropped down in an armchair that had seen better times. Ozzie had bought some of the furniture second-hand from so-called antique stores. This was definitely one such item, its upholstery worn and sagging. But it was still quite comfortable. The thought that it was a chair in which Ozzie often relaxed was also somewhat calming.

I allowed my mind to drift to Ozzie for a moment. He would be so upset if I told him about my find. Maybe I shouldn't tell him, at all. On the other hand, the story would soon spread through the village like wildfire. And even though hardly anybody knew my name, it might come out that it had been a foreigner who had stumbled across the body. Putting one and one together, Ozzie would figure that it had been me, and be even more upset if I kept quiet about this.

I sighed and lifted the mug to my lips. The first sip almost burned my mouth. Well, so much for hoping for a quick warm-up from the inside. I set the mug down on a side table and leaned back, gazing at the empty fireplace across.

The more I thought about the young man, the more I came to the conclusion it had almost looked like an execution. He had faced the killer. So, the killer must have known whom he was shooting. A headshot was never an accident, either. The victim had been selected. The shooter was somebody who knew how to hit a relatively small target. Anybody else – this much I knew from Linda when she had talked about target practice one time – would have gone for a broader one. Such as the chest or the belly. Which also indicated that it had been a seasoned gun person who had wanted their victim dead with no risk of survival.

Why?

Because the killer didn't want to be identified in case the young man had known him or been able to describe him. Or her. Better be safe than sorry.

Large caliber ... I reached for the mug again. This time, I was able to enjoy my tea without running the risk of blistering the roof of my mouth. Large calibers indicated rifles. Not pistols. Not revolvers. Well, my first thought on hearing the shot had been that of hunting. Basically, anybody could be hunting in the area. Though the village was definitely *not* hunting ground. And the prey had been human in this case.

What did a complete cartridge look like anyhow? Would a case of birdshot look different from one that held one single bullet? Also, there was military in the area. Lots of them. Some even just traveled through. Could any of the G.I.s stationed at Mildenhall have been the shooter? Their background seemed almost a guarantee for taking precise aim. Or could it have been one of the few British soldiers in the area?

What were the odds that any person traveling through would have known a Roma who might also just have been traveling through? How would that person have had any idea where to find him? The whole thing indicated a rendezvous. Highly unlikely circumstances. Still, I ought to keep that idea in mind.

The phone rang. Ozzie had an old-fashioned landline with an answering machine, pretty much the same as I had back home. Its display showed me his cellphone number. I almost hyperventilated, not sure whether I was relieved to hear his voice or fretted whether he'd find me out. I lifted the receiver.

"Ozzie, my whiz …"

"Emma, sweetheart. You are sounding a bit breathless. Is everything okay?"

"Yes," I lied. "Why wouldn't it?!"

"*You* tell me!"

"No, everything is fine. How was *your* day, though? You're the one who's travelling, after all."

"Everything is running smooth. I'll take my guys out to a restaurant that I tried the last time I was here. They have fantastic kabobs and tagines, there. And they put up some mean stage shows, too."

"Neat. I might go out tonight as well."

"To *The Bird in the Bush*?"

"Is there any other pub in Ealingham?"

"You could take the truck and drive somewhere else. Mildenhall, Ely, maybe Cambridge, for all I know."

"Nope, not risking this. Left-hand traffic on foot is pretty much all I can deal with right now. And drinking and driving is not what you'd want me to do, either."

"True. But as to driving, you could always give it a try in the village. Hardly any traffic. Easy practicing."

"Yeah, well …"

"Everything okay with the house? Do you find everything you need?"

"Oh, Ozzie, it's not the first time I'm visiting. The only thing that's missing is you."

"Well, can't be helped. Next time will be different."

"I hope so."

"I love you, sweetheart."

"Wait!" I sensed that for him, basically, everything had been said. He knew that I was alright, that the home was in order, and what I was going to do tonight. He was about to hang up.

"What, sweetheart?"

"Tell me, what kind of guns shoot … " I rummaged around for the note I had taken down earlier, "30-06 caliber ammo?"

"The old M-1 Garand. That's a U.S. rifle used in WW II and in Korea. Why? Where does that come from?"

I stayed quiet.

"Emma?" Ozzie's voice had taken on an aggravated tone. "What are you up to now?"

"Nothing." In a way it was true. I had no intention to do anything with any rifle or ammunition. I just wanted to know some facts.

"You are not getting yourself into any strange or dangerous situation, are you?"

I bit my lower lip. "No." I decided that wasn't exactly a lie. A dead person was not dangerous. And I was only researching a little. "I just found an empty bullet case on the dike this afternoon. That's all. It made me curious. Especially, since I have never seen any hunters around here."

"And there shouldn't be." Ozzie fell silent. Then he asked, "Where on the dike?"

"Oh, pretty close to your home, actually," I said lightly. "It just made me curious. If it's a U.S. gun, would that mean that an American soldier could have shot it?"

"Don't be daft," Ozzie said and sounded really angry now. "Sorry. But, no. These semi-automatics have been replaced in the 1970s by a different sort of gun. And there is no way any American military member privately collecting vintage guns could bring their own into this country."

"So, it wouldn't have been shot from an M-1," I concluded.

"Well, anybody can buy an M-1 if they set their mind to it. Or it could have been fired from any hunting rifle that uses this kind of caliber," Ozzie conceded.

"But you wouldn't use it on small animals, would you?" I tried him.

Ozzie laughed mirthlessly. "Why do I have the feeling there is so much more behind your questions, Emma?"

"I just want to know," I insisted.

"Well, I remember the last time you just wanted to know something about horse breeding, you almost got yourself kidnapped and possibly killed."

"This is nothing like it," I protested. "It's just about an empty case, and it simply made me curious."

"Sure," Ozzie sighed. "Listen, big caliber is used for big game and, usually, for long-distance shots. Not for any kind of fowl. You'd find that bird blasted to smithereens and spattered all over the place."

"Thank you," I said. The image of the matter around the shooting victim's head rose before my eyes, and I quickly grabbed one of Ozzie's photos on the table next to me to send my thoughts into a happier direction.

"You ought to go to the police station in Ealingham and tell their constables that you found such a case. They might want to know and look into it."

"Okay," I replied breezily.

"Don't take this too easy," Ozzie warned. "The village and its surroundings are not considered hunting grounds, after all. You are not *supposed* to find anything related to guns. An empty case means that somebody shot in the direct vicinity of the place you found it. The case is discarded from the gun and ends up pretty close, depending on what kind of surface it lands. I'm really not comfortable thinking that there might be a shooter around my home. Especially not when you are staying there all by yourself."

"But there was nobody around. It was just the case."

"Still, promise me that you will let the police know."

"I promise," I said. It was not exactly a lie, either. I had pointed out my find to Sergeant Cameron and, therefore, in a way let him know. I didn't have to let Ozzie know that there was a body involved that had most likely been shot by the projectile that had belonged to the case. Why worry him more than necessary? Most likely, the police would find and arrest the killer before Ozzie even returned from his trip to Northern Africa. There would still be enough time to tell him about my gruesome find. And by then, everything would be water under the bridge, and Ozzie wouldn't even have to spend any energy on being upset.

"Alright," Ozzie wound down our conversation. "Hope you have fun at the pub tonight."

"And you at your restaurant."

"Talk to you tomorrow, sweetheart."

"I love you."

Click.

Ozzie was already gone. And I felt the dusk in the house become even denser and more oppressive. Time to switch on some lights and leave them on while I was gone. Just to make it look as if there was somebody inside the house. I had to have people around me now. This afternoon's images and the implication of a killer with a rifle, still roaming around, were not what I wanted to contemplate in any greater detail. Not here. Not now.

5

About half an hour later – it was shortly before six – I went out again. I had added an extra scarf to my warm coat and cap against the humid cold of the November Fens. This time, I also took my gloves along.

The streetlights had turned on a while ago, casting bizarre shadows on the slope of the dike and the trees in the front yards of the neighborhood. Wafts of fog crept in from the Ouse and wavered above the cobbled street. I hurried past Henry's home and a few other scantly lit cottages and bungalows, averting my face from the spot on the dike where I had found the bullet case. Best not to think of it. I shuddered and was glad when I reached the junction towards Main Street.

Here, the houses were built closer to each other, and the front yards became smaller as the streetlights became seemingly more numerous. But that might have been my imagination playing a trick on me. Maybe I was just glad that I was to encounter other human beings in four minutes or five. Traffic through Ealingham's twisted Main Street would be a bit heavier around this hour of the evening, as well. I was definitely spooked by the earlier events and by being all by myself.

I turned right, towards the center of the village. The sidewalks were narrow, and the field stone walls of the buildings here looked even quainter in the yellowish shine of the overhead street illumination. Farther ahead I could already make out the timber frame of the Queen-Anne-style pub. Its lights shone invitingly through its windows, a golden glow in the dark. I picked up my pace, looking forward to be part of the humming crowd inside and to have whatever pub food might strike my appetite tonight. More people started emerging from their homes, also headed for *The Bird in the Bush*.

When I finally reached its entrance, raucous laughter spilled through the door as soon as I opened it and enveloped me with its carefree vibe. I took a deep breath, then took off my hat and loosened my scarf, looking around. I didn't expect to see any familiar faces, of course. I hadn't stayed with Ozzie that often; his and my work schedule hadn't permitted a lot of mutual visits. The publican wouldn't count me as a regular customer. How much less would I recognize any others?!

Figuring where I might have the best chance of any conversation, I headed towards the bar and managed to find what was obviously the last free stool. No wonder. It looked like the unwanted remnant of a yard sale. Its synthetic leather upholstery had cracks through which the padding burst, and it wobbled, as one leg had lost its rubber shoe. But it was better than standing at the bar until, maybe in a couple of hours, somebody would get up from their stool to stagger home. Certainly better than occupying an entire table all by myself, with nobody striking up a conversation, at all. So, I just sat down at the counter and waited my turn to order something to drink.

"Hi!" The publican had moved right in front of me. I presumed he was in his mid-thirties, therefore a bit younger than I, and he looked at me curiously. "What can I get for you?"

"My friend usually orders for me, so I wouldn't know – do you have any Strongbow?" I asked for my favorite cider brand.

He raised his brows. "Naw. But if it's a rather dry cider you're looking for, our local one on tap is pretty dry, with a hint of pears. And we got another one that's a bit sweeter. Wanna try a sip?"

"Why, that is kind of you!" I exclaimed surprised. "But, no thanks. I think I had the dry one in the past. I'll take a pint." He gave me a short nod and was about to move away. "And the menu, please. I'd love to eat something, too."

"Here at the bar?" he asked.

I nodded. He shrugged and began tapping my cider while taking another order from another customer at the end of the bar.

"Let me guess," I heard a female voice to my left. "You are from Germany?"

My head flew around. The lady who had spoken was quite a bit older than I and looked very respectable in a white blouse and lavender-colored cardigan, her brunette hair combed into a tidy knot. Her hazel eyes scrutinized me without a blink, and she lifted her glass of ale as in a salute.

"Why, yes!" I caught myself staring. She pointed at the bar, indicating that my glass of cider had been placed in front me. I lifted it. "Cheers!" I took a deep sip. The fresh, slightly bitter flavor was quite enjoyable. "Mmmh." Then, "How did you guess?" I licked my lips and set the glass down again.

"Intuition." Her eyes twinkled, but her face stayed unmoved.

"Well, then let me take a guess. You are from London. Or some such place."

"Some such place," she said.

"Well, at least I figured you couldn't be from around here," I grinned. "Your accent is different from how they speak around here."

At this remark, the woman's mouth split into a smile, and I thought I actually heard a subdued giggle.

"I should hope so." Then her face turned sober again. "But you are right, I live in one of the London suburbs, these days." We sat in silence for a moment, and I almost thought the interview was over when she said, "I overheard you ask for the menu. I just arrived here and don't know anybody yet. Mind if I keep you company?"

"Not at all."

"Could we sit at one of the tables, though? I'm never really comfy at a bar. I always feel like that is okay only when you are alone and want to talk to somebody."

"Sure," I said. If she decided to leave later on and I didn't feel like going to my dark and lonely interim home, I could still return to the bar again.

"Barb Tope," she introduced herself and offered her hand. I shook.

"Emma Schwarz," I replied. "Nice to meet you."

"Nice to meet *you*," she smiled. She retrieved her glass and our menus from the bar and took the lead towards a small table by the window.

I followed her against a new stream of incoming patrons and dropped down in a slightly more comfortable wooden chair with armrests. It wasn't a bad place to sit, actually. I was able to look outside, to observe the bar, and to notice pretty much anybody who darkened the door.

"So, what brought you here?" Barb asked. She smoothed her lavender-colored cardigan as she sat down.

"Love", I replied.

"Nice!"

"You?"

"Work," she said.

"To Ealingham, of all places?"

"What's wrong with it?"

"Well, it's only a tiny village," I pondered aloud. "There is nothing much of any employment here, unless you work at the pub, which obviously you don't, at the Londis store next door, or at the elementary school. Well, that is an option. But to come here from London to teach a few little kids reading and arithmetic?"

A waitress appeared at our table. She was a different one from the last time Ozzie and I had been here, at *The Bird in the Bush*.

"Can I take your orders?" she asked. She was in her early twenties, blond and tattooed, and kind of pretty. But her features also betrayed that she would respond to any unsought attention from male customers in an adequate manner. I imagined she could become quite tough when necessary.

"I'd like a chicken and mushroom pie with a side salad, please," I said.

"I'd like to have a grilled cheese sandwich," Barb ordered.

"Sorry," the waitress replied. "Not on the menu. But you could have a ploughman's lunch."

Barb sighed. "It was worth a try. I'll take it. Double cheese, please. And a side salad, also."

The waitress noted it down, took the menus, and sauntered towards the bar to disappear in the kitchen door behind it.

"I always give it a try," Barb explained her order. "When I was a kid, my parents took me to Disneyworld in Orlando, Florida. It didn't impress me much. I knew that the princesses weren't the real deal, and Goofy wasn't half as cute as I had imagined him. But they had grilled cheese sandwiches at one of their restaurants. And, boy, didn't I eat my fill?! My mother had to recreate them after we returned home again. But somehow, they never tasted the same way. Still, they were better than nothing.

Anyhow, ever since I've been earning my own living, I have been giving it a try at any pub and tavern I go."

I laughed. "Such as in *Constant dripping wears the stone*?"

"Exactly. Who knows? At one point, somebody might finally relent and put them on their menu." We laughed. "Meanwhile, I'm either offered ploughman's lunches or mac 'n' cheeses. I guess, I've become quite the expert on either."

"You could write an article on this aspect of the British cuisine for a culinary magazine," I suggested.

"I don't think anybody would want to read that, though," Barb said with a wink. "Writing anything but bald facts isn't my forte. – But you … do you like to write?"

"It's the way I make my living. I'm a journalist."

"Oh?"

"Small daily paper in my hometown. Mostly cultural and social stories. – What about *your* job? You keep me guessing."

Barb leaned slightly forward and kind of spoke through the corner of her mouth, "So, it *was* you who found the body, wasn't it?"

I was totally taken aback. "What?!" I whispered. "What do you mean?!"

"Oh, come on, Emma," Barb said, and suddenly I knew what kind of a job she had. "I was briefed as I was driving up here to take over the case. Plain good luck that I have been running into you immediately after my arrival. I just needed to make sure that it really *was* you."

"You are Scotland Yard?" I whispered and felt my blood drain from my face.

"That's what we are called in detective fiction, yes."

"Oh yes, I remember. I heard it is officially called Criminal Something Something."

"Criminal Investigation Department, yes," Barb helped me out.

"Right, and that was pretty quick. Your arrival here, I mean."

"Well, we are dealing with a very suspicious murder that involves one of Britain's ethnic minorities. Which will cause much attention with the media and, therefore, the public if it's not investigated promptly and as visibly as possible." Barb leaned back, lifted her glass, and emptied it in one single draft. It was pretty astonishing how she seemed to be such a lady, on the one hand, but also to have a tougher side to her. Well, as an officer with Britain's best of police force, she'd better.

"Ethnic minority …" An image of the young man's body flashed through my mind. His swarthy skin.

"Well, it must have struck you that he didn't have exactly the pallor of an English rose."

"No! No, of course."

"We are still not sure about his identity. But we are pretty sure that he belongs to the greater Romany community."

I stayed quiet. Yes, that figured. Maybe that was what had seemed somewhat familiar about him. He had reminded me of the fortune teller Linda had consulted in Newmarket a few days ago. But there had been something else that I couldn't fathom yet. Still, I had to let Barb know.

"Some of them seem to be living in their winter quarters near Ealingham. And the other day, a friend of mine and I were in Newmarket – a fortune teller has set up her wagon there."

Barb nodded quietly and didn't let on what she was thinking. Meanwhile, our waitress returned with a plate full of bread, cheese, butter, mustard, pickled onions, and gherkins in one hand and, in the other, a plate full of a rectangular pie with a few decorative slits in the top to let out the steam. She set both in front of us.

"Could I have another Beck's, please?" Barb requested.

"Sure," the waitress said, although I could see that she'd have preferred it if Barb had gone over to the bar and taken care of business herself.

Barb wasn't oblivious either. She winked at me after the girl had turned her back. "She's a feisty one, I'm sure. She better know who has more pull, in case of doubt."

"They know who you are?"

"Of course," Barb laughed grimly. "When the village constable books you a room at this place because they don't like me in their field of work. I'm pretty sure, he let off steam about me before I even arrived here."

"So, they also know about the ... dead person?" I couldn't bring myself to name the young man a corpse or a body. Suddenly, knowing that he belonged to the Romany people, he was more of a person to me than a case.

"Not sure how much he told them about the case. But actually, since he is clearly still a rookie, he'll stick to all the rules and won't confide in anybody outside the forces about the case."

I nodded. "He didn't have any ID on him?" I wondered aloud.

Barb shook her head. "Nothing. A cell phone that we try to figure out. It's locked." Then she leaned forward again. I thought she might want to dig into her food, and I attacked my pie with knife and fork, overcome by hunger all of a sudden. But as I stuffed a bite into my mouth and almost burnt its roof because of the piping-hot filling, Barb whispered, "I know you also found an empty bullet case on the dike."

I almost choked. "Yep," I managed to say in between coughs. "What about it?"

"This area is not known as a hunting ground for big game, is it?"

"I presume that nobody was supposed to fire any weapon in the village and surroundings, in the first place," I said, now with my mouth empty.

"No, of course not." Barb stabbed at a silver onion with her fork and took it off the prongs with her lips only. She chewed pensively, visibly enjoying the flavors, and swallowed. "What *do* you know about hunting around here?"

"Nothing much," I parried. "Remember that I'm only here on a visit."

"Where is your host anyway? Why are you alone in here?" Barb sounded as if she already knew.

"He's currently deployed, and I'm his house-sitter." I felt as if I sounded defiant. As if I had to provide an alibi for him.

Barb nodded. "One of the Americans stationed over in Mildenhall, I presume?"

I nodded and doggedly kept eating my pie.

"You know about the caliber of the case. Sergeant Cameron briefed me about you and your find. And he admitted that he told you it was a 30-06. I'll also tell you it was a full metal jacket; the brand doesn't really matter. It's the kind some very specific U.S. rifles shoot. So, don't be surprised. We are looking into anybody who is stationed over there and used to frequent this pub until last night."

"Well, Ozzie … that is, my friend left here on Monday already." Barb lifted her eyes from her plate expectantly. "So, he is above suspicion. You'll have to look into somebody else. Maybe the publican remembers somebody with a conspicuous attitude."

"If *you* remember anyone particularly, just let me know. You know where to find me. And you better save my phone number in your smartphone."

"Flip phone," I said lamely.

"Whichever," she replied and made it a point that I copy her number into my cell under her very eyes, immediately.

Suddenly, I felt the urge to be ahead of the police investigation. I didn't like any of Ozzie's fellow countrymen in the focus of suspicion. Especially, since none of them were supposed to have any private arms over here. I just needed proof to clear them. And therefore, I had to find who had really committed the murder.

6

We changed subjects and began to chat about more personal but uncontroversial topics. Barb had been to Germany as a kid, and she was keen to know how things had changed in my mother country. I had always loved Great Britain and couldn't get enough of what treasures I might want to explore over here yet. She said she wanted to go visit the Munich Oktoberfest so badly. Just once. I told her that I'd never really experienced Brighton or Liverpool. She said she remembered Paderborn as a quaint town with a beautiful pedestrian zone. I told her how I had fallen in love with the city of Norwich at first sight. Barb dreamed up a storm of German food, especially Wiener Schnitzel. I had to concede that the British cuisine had changed for so much better that it didn't deserve its bad reputation any longer. Thus, we finished our dinner on a very pleasant note, even though I had tucked away a note in my mind that I had to find out more about the killed Roma.

"I've had a long day," Barb finally yawned behind her right hand after she had paid and tipped the waitress generously. "I guess I'll call it a day and go to my room upstairs. See you around."

She rose, stretched, gave me a little wave, and walked to a doorway at the back that led to a staircase. I decided I'd hang around a bit longer. But I'd do so at the bar. So, I grabbed my coat, scarf, hat, and handbag, and moved over. By now, the bar was crowded with people – farmers discussing the latest market regulations, sports fans watching a rugby game that was on screen above the bar, muted, a few girls in their twenties, obviously on the look-out for a flirt or maybe something more. Some kind, older guys moved enough, so I was able to squeeze in and order another beverage.

Strange how sitting and having a meal even with a stranger could make a room more comfortable and familiar. And how, when you were alone again, the former warmth seemed a bit reduced and the confidence you had had was diminished. At least, that was the way I felt right now. Or maybe I was just overwrought by the events earlier and somewhat lonesome without Ozzie.

"You on the wagon, girl, or what?" an American voice drawled into my ear. I turned around and found myself face to face with the same guy who had tried to connect with the girl I had observed handing over the envelope to the publican a few nights ago. What a coincidence!

"Not really," I answered and bent a bit backward. The guy was a bit too close for my comfort. "Is that your usual pick-up line?"

"It could work, couldn't it?" He was leering at me now. He was not a bad-looking guy. But being drunk didn't make him exactly attractive, either.

"Didn't work with the brown-skinned girl the other day, did it?"

He looked at me cluelessly, and I realized that he didn't remember her scornful glance. He wouldn't remember me, either. He was in a world of his own.

"Ey, March!" the publican shouted from the other end of the bar where he was serving a couple two almost overflowing pints. "Leave that lady alone, will ya?"

The guy – whose name was obviously March – lifted his hands in apology and backed off. "I didn't do anything. Really."

"Well, but I know you were about to lay hands on somebody who doesn't belong to you. Got that talent, don't you?"

The guy grumbled something and withdrew into a corner where he leaned against a pillar, and stared gloomily at the crowd.

"You okay?" The publican had finished his business with the patrons he'd been serving, and now he was facing me. I nodded. "He isn't a bad guy. Just gets into people's faces lately. Got a *Dear John* letter from his girl in the U.S., and now he is a bit lost. Nothing that won't blow over eventually."

"Oh." I hadn't expected to get to hear the story of March's life.

"Seems he always goes for ladies who are already going steady with somebody. You're Ozzie's girl, aren't you?"

So, he *had* noticed me, after all, but never let on. I took him in a bit closer. He had a ruddy face, reddish-brown, very short hair, and blue eyes, was stocky in built, and seemed to be at peace with the world and himself. He saw my astonishment and chuckled. "If you are behind the bar all day, you get to see a lot.

And you put one and one together. Ozzie is a regular here, as you probably know. Mostly just dinner and a pint on his evenings off. He told me about you. Emma it is, right?" I nodded. "Alan," he smiled.

"Hi, Alan. And thanks for the rescue."

"De nada. What can I get you?"

"A glass of Sprite, no ice, please. Don't want to end up drunk. – So, this March guy – how will he get home?"

"Oh, he lives in the village. He'll be fine. Somebody will probably be kind enough and walk him to his front door."

"I've seen him behave similarly the other night when I was here with Ozzie. He tried to chat up a pretty girl with quite the Mediterranean looks. She held her own."

Alan's face darkened while he was tapping my Sprite. "That was a real bad move. She's not for him, that's for sure."

"Because she goes steady with somebody?"

Alan shook his head and placed the glass in front of me. Some of the soda sloshed over the brim. "Sorry about that. Nope. That's not the only reason. It's just better to leave the Roma alone. Especially their girls."

"Why is that?"

"It just means trouble," Alan muttered. "Different culture. We simply don't mix."

He nodded abruptly and turned to another customer who waved an empty glass over the bar.

I was dumbfounded. For one, I didn't have the impression that Alan was treating any of his customers in discriminating or disrespectful ways. And I *had* seen him interact with the girl in ways that suggested that he knew her. In a confidential way. So, what business did *he* have with her? Because business it had seemed. He had served as a go-between, hadn't he?

The next few minutes were very busy for Alan, as a new group had entered the pub to have a nightcap. He was tapping one glass after another, carefully taking his time where the foam needed to settle, so a pint would be a true pint when served. I wondered how he managed to keep all the orders in his head, share a joke here and remark something there to customers, and still get it right when pushing the glasses towards the patrons.

Finally, everybody seemed to have settled with their beverage, and he saw me gaze at him. He lifted his chin. "Another drink for you?"

I shook my head. "No. But wondering whether you have an answer to a question of mine."

He came over, curious. "Depends on the question."

"When I hear shooting, what kind of game do hunters go for here in the area?"

"Oh, waterfowl, I guess." He scratched his chin. "It's hunting season right now. So, you might hear quite some of that in the entire region. But only from far away."

"So, there are no hunting grounds close by?"

"Well, there is an estate about five miles away. They offer hunting classes and hunting outings. I heard of grouse and pheasant hunts in their park. Maybe rabbits as well. If you want some bigger game, they charter a mini-bus to get the group into an area farther north where there are deer, I heard. And there are quite a few other country seats in the area where they do similar. Why?"

"So, there is no hunting at the boundaries of Ealingham? Or within?"

Alan's eyes widened with wonder. "Are you kidding me?! Just imagine if anybody went around the village, wielding a gun to shoot waterfowl or as much as the bunny in their garden. No! Unheard of! It would endanger everybody around. And where would you draw the line?! This side of the river Ouse? The other bank?"

I just listened and watched his upset. Was it real? Or was he a good actor?

"So, you are telling me that shooting guns never happens outside restricted areas such as estates and specifically assigned countryside?"

"Why are you even asking this?! Do you mean anybody has been shooting? I mean ..."

At this moment, there was some commotion behind me, and I turned to search for the cause. The crowd parted to let through a very frantic-looking young woman. I blinked. Was it her? She was dressed in a dark anorak and a dark blue knitted hat.

Except for her somewhat foreign features, she would not have stood out against anybody in this crowd. Except for her wild eyes and the silent scream written on her face. I took a deep, careful breath – it was the young woman whom I had happened to observe barely a week ago when she had handed over her letter to Alan.

The young woman basically sank against the bar, breathless, her hands on the counter. Her mouth was a toneless cry, her eyes started to well over. Her frame was shaking, and she seemed pretty close to a breakdown. Alan, who had turned to serve some other customers, just lifted a hand as in asking her to wait or to come behind the bar or both. His face had lost color, and he was frowning. The girl's fingertips had turned white in gripping the countertop. Seeing Alan gesture towards her, her limp body straightened again with purpose, and she pushed herself off to struggle her way through the crowd, past me, towards the side of the bar. Alan hurried over as fast as he could after counting out change for his patrons, then hugged her and pulled her to the kitchen entrance. Not mixing with them, right? Yet he had definitely put his arms around her. What was going on?

I strained my ears but couldn't hear anything over the din around me. I could barely make out their voices. It was impossible for me to follow them into the kitchen, of course. I could hardly saunter behind the bar. And trying to figure any back access to the kitchen was equally useless. By the time I would have found any, the conversation inside might have been finished.

The only thing I could do was to wait until Alan came back. But he didn't. One of the barmaids took over for him.

"Was that Alan's girlfriend?" I asked, seemingly innocent. "Is she alright?"

The girl just raised her eyebrows. "Alan has no girlfriend. Not that I know of. And Rose is a kitchen help. No idea what this is about. But I'm sure she's taken care of. – Another pint?"

"No, thanks. I guess I better call it a night."

I finished my Sprite and placed the glass on the counter. Then I settled my tab, slipped into my coat, and pensively walked towards the door. One last look over my shoulder showed me that nothing had changed. The crowd was loud and chummy, the barmaid's head was barely visible behind the bar, and neither Alan nor Rose had returned.

I stepped outside and was hit by a blast of cold November air. The fog had thickened, and the streetlights cut through it with cylindric beams. Traffic had died down to almost nothing, and some of the lights in the old houses around had already been switched off.

So, Rose was not just any girl but an employee. And she seemed to have an issue that Alan knew about. Alan, who had advised me that one better left the Roma alone. Only *he* didn't. And when he had said that they meant trouble, had he meant Rose's trouble in particular?

7

"I knew I shouldn't have left you behind but grabbed you by your arm and dragged you back home to Filderlingen!" Linda's voice sounded way too loud and awake in my ears. "And why do you sound so strange?"

"Ah'm tshusht brusha ma teeh …" I lifted my mug to the lips to rinse my mouth. After spitting out the foamy mess, I ran my wet hand over my mouth, dried it with a towel, took a quick look in the mirror, and pulled a face at myself.

"What?! You're brushing your teeth?! Are you getting up only now?! It's nine o'clock. Every self-respecting person in the world is up by that time."

"It's an hour earlier over here, remember? Plus, I'm on vacation."

Linda sighed. "My bad. Sorry. Shall I call you later again?"

"Nope." I rubbed cold cream on my face, took my flip phone, and walked out of the bathroom and over to the master bedroom to dress. "What's this about anyhow?" I placed the phone on Ozzie's nightstand and slipped into woolen socks, jeans, and a thick off-white sweater.

"I got a call from Niko."

"So? You are supposed to get calls from Niko whenever there is a crime story that looks like bigger news on which to follow up."

"Well, there is a crime story, alright. But Niko sure didn't get it from me."

I walked over to the kitchen to toast some bread and boil water for a cup of filter coffee. "That means you hadn't heard of it yet and it wasn't on the police blotter?! That's rare."

"It's more than rare. It's terrible!" Linda sounded really upset.

"Well, tell them that not even you can be in the know of everything. Maybe it happened afterhours?"

"No," Linda snapped. "It didn't even happen in my territory."

"Well, then why did Niko call *you* of all people?!"

"Argh! Because it concerns *you*, my friend! Does Ozzie know already that you found a body?"

"Oh my! Is that what it is about?!"

"Very much so. So, does Ozzie know already?"

"No. Why should he?"

"Well, you are on the phone with each other every day, as far as I know."

"So?"

"Have you told him?"

I rolled my eyes. The water was boiling by now, and I hadn't even put a filter into the filter cone on top of my breakfast mug.

"No, I haven't. And I won't."

I struggled with the bag of filters, pulled one out while clamping the phone between my cheek and shoulder, and stuck it into the cone. Then I opened a can of ground coffee and spooned the stuff generously into the filter.

"You won't." Linda sounded as if she were hyperventilating by now. "How can you *not* tell him?!"

"Very simply because it wouldn't change a thing. It wouldn't make me unfind the body. It wouldn't make the young man alive again. It wouldn't bring Ozzie home."

"You are impossible."

"Whatever," I said but didn't feel as nonchalant. "But how come that Niko knows about this?"

"Well, guess what. They needed to verify your identity and checked up on your background."

"They …" Then it dawned on me. "Wait a second. Do you mean that Barb What's-her-last-name from Scotland Yard actually went over my contact info and my statement, figured out where to find my workplace, and got Niko on the phone?!"

"Pretty much. He must have been the first of your colleagues at the office this morning. And he got an earful of your adventure. He was shocked. So was I when he called me and told me straight away. He asked me to ask you to come home immediately."

I laughed. And because my hand was shaking, I spilled some hot water that was meant to go over the ground coffee in the filter over my other hand.

"Ouch! Shoot!" I yelled.

"What happened?"

"Shouldn't make breakfast while on the phone with you."

"Did you cut yourself?"

"No, burned my hand." I rushed over to the sink and let some cold water run over the already reddening skin on my left hand. "Darn, that hurts."

"Well, hope it heals quickly," Linda said, somewhat empathetic. "Anyhow, are you?"

"What?!"

"Coming home?"

"Of course, I'll be coming home," I said and began losing my patience. "I never intended to stay here longer than my vacation lasts. And no, I won't come home early just because I found this body, if that was the question."

A long sigh and silence. Then, "Well, I tried. Just promise me that you will stay safe and keep away from the body."

I was able to safely promise Linda that much. I was pretty sure I wouldn't encounter the body ever again. By now it would be in a cooler somewhere in a pathological institute for whatever purposes they had in mind there. The cause of death was pretty obvious, I thought. But, of course, somebody had to identify John Doe yet. There was probably no open coffin before the funeral. I wasn't even sure whether there would be a funeral of which I'd be notified for participation. So, I solemnly promised Linda, yes, I'd keep away from the body.

"Good," she stated. And I didn't contradict her. "Now something else – Steffen and I have been thinking about getting married on horseback. Isn't that romantic?!"

"Well, it's certainly quite unusual," I admitted. "Does your pastor also have to be seated on a horse? Or will he have to crank his neck and squint into the sun while he is reading you the wedding vows?"

"Oh, we already made sure that he is also at home in the saddle," Linda reassured me. "We had just thought that maybe you …"

"No!"

My answer shot out of my mouth before I could even think. That's what's instinct is about. Although I had been around horses willy-nilly last spring when I had investigated that series of arson cases on horse farms, I was still not comfortable around these huge creatures. They didn't freak me out anymore. But I couldn't claim that I particularly trusted them either. Who knew what was going on in those big heads with those, admittedly, beautiful eyes and large, soft muzzles?

"You'd just have to sit still and …"

"No," I repeated. "I know that something bad would happen – somebody would sneeze, my horse would bolt, and I'd be flung in the air. No way!"

I heard Linda exhale. "Well, it was worth the try."

"Why can't you just do a very pretty and classic chapel wedding and do a horse thing for show later at Solitude Palace? I'm sure a whole lot of other people would appreciate it, too."

"Party pooper," Linda grumbled.

"I'm just thinking of the elderly people who wouldn't be able to run in case somebody sneezed and …"

"I get the picture," Linda interrupted. "I'll talk it over with Steffen. I wanted something extraordinary."

"Well, you know what I think about extraordinary things and weddings."

"And what would that be?"

"The more it is about the wedding, the less it is about the marriage."

"Duh. You know us better than that."

"I should hope so."

My stomach began to growl, and I eyed my orange marmalade toast yearningly. "Listen, I got to go now. I have to answer this body's needs." The instant I uttered the term "body" I rued it. And, indeed, Linda jumped on it instantly.

"By the way, Niko said that Detective Superintendent Tope also asked whether you covered any crime stories. He didn't exactly lie when he said no. But he didn't tell her the exact truth about your sleuthing in the arson case either. So, you better tread carefully around her, you hear me?"

"He did that? I like him better and better."

"Not funny, Emma. This time neither he nor I are around if you get yourself into a ditch again. So, you better don't even think of it."

"I don't," I replied quickly. Of course, I didn't want to think of myself in a ditch, scout's honor.

"Good. Well, I'll let you go then. Is it one of these amazing English breakfasts you are making for yourself?"

"Nope. Just toast with a bit of marmalade, coffee, and a glass of juice."

"Sounds frugal."

"It's exactly what I want this morning."

"Say hi to Ozzie for me."

"Will do," I said, my mouth already crammed with a first bite of deliciously sweet, sour, and bitter crunchy toast.

Click.

I was free to go. I swallowed. Oh Linda, my dear friend, I didn't lie to you. But neither did I tell you the exact truth …

8

People's actions are often based on contradiction. Prohibit somebody something, and they are almost sure to find it even more interesting than it really is. In this case, I had plenty of warning advice if not prohibition thrown into my path. But it wasn't this fact that enhanced my curiosity even more. I *knew* that curiosity killed the cat and that, in the case of a first-degree murder, I had to tiptoe around what proof I might find. Even what I had found so far would probably endanger me.

As Detective Superintendent Barb Tope had pointed out, the Criminal Investigation Department were looking in a direction that was highly unlikely and that might cause somebody severe career problems though they might turn out to be innocent. Even the slightest shade of doubt can destroy a person's reputation, after all. There was no way that one of Ozzie's compatriots could have committed the crime. I simply had to interfere and see whether I was able to find out something more. Something better. Something that pointed in the right direction.

Therefore, after what Linda had perceived as a scant breakfast but had actually hit the spot, I put on my bad-weather gear and walked over to Henry's place. I knocked on the door and had to wait a considerate while until he opened.

Henry was yet unshaven and squinted at me, bewildered. He uttered something that I translated to, "Goodness, it's not the afternoon yet, is it?!"

"Hi Henry," I smiled sheepishly. "I know it's way early. And I will take Rocky for another walk this afternoon. But could I borrow him for a little just now? Please?"

Meanwhile, Rocky's fine ears must have picked up my voice, for I heard a short yelp, and then he rushed from behind Henry through the gap between the man and the doorframe to greet me with a pounce that almost toppled me over. Henry grabbed his collar just in time to soften the impact and cussed at the lively Labrador. Then he said something utterly incomprehensible to me, told Rocky to sit, and turned his back on me to vanish into the dark hallway of his home. Rocky, seeing that his master was gone, raised himself immediately and approached me, whining and wagging. I patted the cutsie. A few minutes later, Henry returned with Rocky's leash, hooked it in place, and handed it over to me.

"I won't be very long," I promised. "Maybe an hour or so."

He mumbled something, then gave me a tiny wave, turned, and closed the door behind himself.

Rocky looked up at me expectantly. Before he could finish walking around me and tying me up with his leash, I took a step towards the road.

"Come on, my friend!"

Rocky followed me eagerly. Soon he was happily straining against the leash as usual, and I had to walk fast in order to keep up without strangling him. He knew that we were headed for the towpath, as we had gone there all of the past afternoons. We passed through the floodgate in the dike. Today, the sun was trying hard to break through the gray morning clouds. The wetlands on the other side of the river Ouse were looking lush and were glistening with last night's dew. Only the cattails with their frazzled heads at the fringe of the water betrayed that it was late fall.

I turned into our usual direction on the path, and Rocky started sniffing curiously at anything that seemed vaguely interesting. A bollard on this side of the path, the seatless remnants of a bench on the other. I watched him, amused, although I felt tension rise in me. Did I really go back to the place where I had found the body yesterday? What if there were still remains of some sort? Just the thought of it made my stomach roil. But if I wanted to find out anything helpful for the small American minority under suspicion for all the wrong reasons right now, I had to overcome my nauseous thoughts.

Was the leash working like a telephone line? Rocky began to sense my worry and looked at me more and more often as if in doubt whether he should continue doing what he was doing. Or maybe I was just imagining it. Maybe he was just waiting to be let off the leash. But not today. Not on this stretch of the towpath. I didn't want him to run off onto the crime scene and disturb anything. I didn't want him to cause me any trouble.

As we were approaching the bend in the path, Rocky sat down and started whining. Maybe he remembered what he had discovered less than 24 hours ago. Maybe he was just tired because I never took him for any walks in the morning. I also felt tension rise; a shiver crept over my back and made my hair stand up. Not literally, of course. My ponytail was still in place. I tugged at Rocky's leash.

"Come on, boy. Don't be scared. There is nothing to be afraid of."

As soon as we turned around the bend, we had to stop. Crime scene tape was spanned across the path, and there were four men in white overalls all over the place between this tape and that on the other side of the area. They had cut some of the high grass on the river bank. And now they were scanning seemingly every inch of the ground with metal detectors. It made sense. Whatever they were looking for would be found more easily in the shorter vegetation.

"I should have listened to Sergeant Cameron," I heard a familiar voice by my left shoulder. "He told me that you would return to the crime scene without fail. That you were just this kind of person."

"Good morning, Barb," I said without turning. "Did you sleep well last night?"

"As sound as a baby," she replied. "Thank you."

Only now did I look at her. She was smiling grimly under a pastel-green knitted hat that complimented her eyes and made them look even more hazel.

"It's not forbidden to walk along the towpath unless one trespasses beyond the tape, right?" I was angry with myself as I heard the defense in my tone.

"No, of course not."

For a while we stood there in silence. It was a bit like a competition about who could stand and watch longer without saying a word. We both wanted answers. Only, whereas I knew that was the case with Barb, she could only surmise that I was after the backstory to the murder, too. In the end, Barb broke the silence.

"What are you really doing here? You are not just taking a walk. You are looking for something, aren't you?"

"Closure," I ventured. It was part of the truth, for sure.

"Closure," Barb repeated and gazed straight ahead. "That's a big word for someone who has found a body. Do you need any psychological support? I could try and help find you some."

"No, thanks. – Has it ever happened to you?"

"What? Finding a dead body?"

"Yes."

"I wish." I gasped. "Don't misunderstand me. A lot of crime sites would stay undisturbed and let me come to conclusions way sooner because of the evidence I would find way faster. It's certainly not that I'm keen on finding a murder victim myself."

I nodded, still staring at the crime site where one of the men had apparently gotten a signal from his metal detector. It turned out to be an empty beer can, though, and was discarded into a small pile of other metal trash.

"It's a shame how people litter," Barb observed. "They keep forgetting that the world is like one big living room. In the end, it's as if they tossed all that stuff inside their own homes. Strangely enough, they probably keep *those* spic and span, though."

"What are they looking for anyhow?" I dared to ask.

"The bullet."

"Why would that help?"

"Each gun has something like an individual fingerprint inside their barrels. When the bullet is shot, it carries these specific traits." Barb sighed. "It's still like looking for a needle in the haystack if you have that as the only evidence."

"So, the so-called fingerprints are not listed in any database?" I asked, astonished.

"Even if they were, there are guns that would have been manufactured outside the timeframe when such a database was built. Or in other countries."

"True," I conceded. "So, you simply keep the bullet with the other evidence you have?"

"We do. But meanwhile we are searching for the person who might own the respective gun."

"Do you already know the identity of the young man?" I asked cautiously.

I didn't want to upset Barb. I knew it must be kind of a question of honor to her to figure out such important details as fast as possible. I stuffed my cold hands into my coat pockets. Again, I had forgotten my gloves. Rocky reacted to the movement at the end of the leash with hopeful eyes. He must be bored just to be sitting in one place, watching something that might offer some excitement for him, too.

"Nothing yet. We will ask around with a head shot." Barb grimaced. "No pun intended. But I'm not sure whether we'll get results anytime soon. If he was a Roma, as I suspect, his fellow people might clam up as soon as police shows up to ask."

"I might help," I offered maybe a bit too quickly.

Barb raised her eyebrows so they almost vanished under the rim of her hat. "You will do no such thing. I'm a plain clothes detective and can handle this very well." She lifted the tape now and slipped under it to the other side as if signaling that our conversation was over.

"Sorry," I muttered.

Barb relented. "Listen, this is a murder case. The killer is still out there and most likely on tenterhooks about what we might find, how soon we'll find it, and what we will make of it. Somebody who shoots somebody in the head is cold-blooded and prone to defend their freedom with another round. You don't even want to get near them. That's *my* job. Okay?"

"Yes, Ma'am."

Barb gave me little wave and strode towards the men in overalls.

"Found anything useful?"

I wasn't able to hear anything but the sound of a man's voice and then hers replying. Rocky got up and tried to get to the other side of the tape, too.

"You stay here, my friend." I pulled the leash in more tightly, and Rocky plopped down again, frustrated.

Over by the bank of the Ouse, one of the men seemed to have found something that caught his attention. He called Barb over and pointed at something on the ground. She bent, and then her body hid the rest of what was happening. But when she rose, she placed a small bag into her coat pocket, looked at me over her shoulder, and gave me a sharp nod.

"The bullet?" I mouthed. But she had already returned her attention to the man and discussed something with him.

So, now it was a matter of whether the bullet they had just retrieved and the case I had found yesterday matched in size. And still, even if so, that wouldn't get them an inch closer to the solution. Not until they had found the gun from which it had been fired, and then some. There must be other hints as to the killer.

My mind turned back to the victim. I frowned. What had struck me as familiar about the body? It hadn't been his face – I had never encountered any Roma recently, other than the woman in Newmarket.

"Before you travel to another world for good, beware of bullets."

Had she really been a clairvoyant? I racked my brain. The killer had struck only after she had told me this. She wasn't able to connect me to Ealingham unless Linda had blabbed about me inside the wagon. Unlikely, though, as it had been about *her*, not me. Also, the woman wouldn't have been able to know about my walks with Rocky on the towpath. And how would she have known about the murder? And me finding the body? No. There were obviously really some unfathomable things between heaven and earth. I took a deep breath. It was quite unnerving that the Roma had connected a bullet and me. Plural. Bullets. I shuddered. And I could only hope that with the travel to another world she didn't mean I would be killed. By a bullet, at that.

I shook my head to clear it from the images that crept into my mind. Forget about the warning. Let's focus on the Romany man again. What was it that …

Suddenly it struck me, visualizing his clothing once more. There had been one item that was highly unlikely to have belonged to him. The colorful scarf with this folkloristic pattern. Not just any scarf either. Because I had seen it before.

"Barb!" I called out, standing tiptoes as if that helped any, and my voice squeaked with excitement. I cleared my throat and tried again. "Barb!!!"

I watched the man to whom she was talking move his head in my direction as if he pointed at me with his chin. Barb turned around, visibly annoyed. I must have disturbed her train of thought. But I gestured urgently for her to come over. I simply had to share what observation I had made. Barb said something to the man, and I figured she might have rolled her eyes. She took her time coming over across the wet grass and, finally, positioned herself a couple of yards away, indicating that I was not welcome to join her team. Maybe, she was also upset that I had called her by her first name and not by her title.

"What now? Are you still here?!"

"I have found something."

"What? Where?"

"No, let me reword it. I have found out something. Have you seen any photos of the young man yet?"

"I have. I told you that I think he is a Roma. So, what's this about?"

"Well, he held a bright scarf in one of his hands, right?"

"Yes. It is in the evidence vault along with other items that belonged to him. We assume that he may have held on to the scarf as the woman it belonged to tore away and ran from him. Probably a Romany woman, as the scarf has a typical pattern and the colors also indicate an ethnic minority."

I breathed hard. "Barb, you wouldn't believe it, but I think I know the woman to whom the scarf belongs."

"What?" Barb's eyes grew wide.

"You heard me. I think I have seen the same scarf on a woman I have seen before. Here in Ealingham. At *The Bird in the Bush*."

9

Barb stood openmouthed for a moment.

"Did you know this all along? Or did this just pop up in your mind?"

I blushed and cringed. "I know it sounds a bit strange. I thought there was something familiar about the body. It only struck me now that it was not the body but the one item that didn't make sense with the clothing. A woman's scarf in a dead man's hand. And I had to remember where I had seen it before. About a week ago. When I was at the pub with Ozzie. I mean …"

"Yeah, your friend." Barb hesitated for a moment. "What else do you have? I know that there is more. You look the part."

"Her name is Rose. I don't know the last name. She works at the pub. As a kitchen help, I understand."

Barb stayed quiet for a moment, her eyes staring at a place beyond my shoulders. Then she decided, "You stay here until I'm done with this. Then you come along with me. I want to make sure that you are not going on an excursion by yourself."

She turned around and strode towards the men to discuss something with them, darting me a glance over her shoulder, every once in a while. Then, finally, she returned.

"Let's go. I want to talk to that girl. Rose, you said?" She passed underneath the tape and kept walking.

I nodded and fell in step with her, Rocky keenly pulling on the leash. "I saw her again last night. Very shortly. She came into the pub after you had gone upstairs already and vanished into the kitchen with Alan." Barb barely turned her face towards me. "That's the publican's name," I hastened to add. "I don't know his last name either."

"Not a perfect job for a journalist," Barb taunted me slightly, and the corners of her mouth twitched.

"Well, I wasn't there as a journalist," I countered. "Just as a guest like everybody else. To know Alan's first name was good enough for me, for the time being. I was not going to write an article titled *The Life and Times of a Suffolk Publican*, was I?"

Barb's eyes twinkled as if she enjoyed our sparring. I was not sure I did, though. I was aware that we were able to help each other solve the case. But I was not supposed to be in on it.

"So, you found the bullet, huh?" I ventured finally.

"Yep."

I was a bit breathless, walking briskly and talking at the same time. Barb seemed way more athletic than I. Or maybe she was cleverer, making it seem that way in just uttering few words. Anyhow, she had me on the defensive again, and I didn't like it.

"Do you already have any suspicion as to the killer?"

"We still have to find the gun and will follow it through."

"You'll search in vain. There are all kinds of guns that shoot a caliber 30-06."

"We'll search till we've found it," Barb insisted.

"By then, all other traces may have gone cold, and you might still not have found the killer, only the weapon."

Barb halted all of a sudden. Her hazel eyes were gleaming like coals now and seared right into mine.

"Listen, Emma, I'm not here to discuss the methods of my investigation with you."

I lifted my hands in apology. "I didn't mean to upset you. I just want to save you the trouble to get access to any commander at RAF Mildenhall. I asked Ozzie about the guns yesterday already."

Barb listened, arms akimbo. "So, I might still want to hear it from the horse's mouth that it's none of theirs who shot this young man."

"It could have been the girl …"

"Sure."

"After she tore herself away and left the scarf in the hands …"

"Don't be daft. If she had had a gun on her, do you think the guy would have gone for the scarf instead of the gun?"

"True."

We walked on in silence.

"At least, we could agree that Rose must have known the man. He had her scarf."

Barb gave a short, desperate laugh. "So, if I find an item in the road, does that make me know the owner of the item automatically?"

"You mean he might just have found it? Maybe lying in the towpath?"

"I'm not suggesting anything. I want facts," Barb stated.

We had passed the gate in the dike. We dropped off Rocky at his home. Henry had opened the mouth to ask something when he glimpsed Barb next to me, but I just waved lightly and, then, ignored him. There was no time for explanations. We promptly steered back to the junction that led towards the village center and passed its cobblestone houses that huddled together behind their minimalist front yards. We finally reached Main Street. Traffic was denser than usual.

Barb squinted at the cars driving by. "Do you know anybody renting vehicles around here?"

"You might want to try in Mildenhall," I replied. "Or Ely."

Barb quietly nodded. "Sounds plausible." She gazed at her watch. "Half past ten."

I didn't answer anything. If I were her, I'd presume that breakfast at *The Bird in the Bush* was over by now, and the kitchen helps were all in to prep lunch and take care of the breakfast dishes.

The center of the village looked every bit as picturesque as a postcard this morning. Minus a blue sky. The village green was well-kempt, it's lawn immaculately cropped. There was a world war memorial in its center, decorated with a wreath of red textile poppies. The perpendicular church stood across from the pub, and the police station across from the town hall. There was a certain logic to the grid with all of these institutions at the center and in walking distance from each other.

Barb marched energetically towards the door of the pub. She tore it open and didn't even check whether I was following her immediately or not. She didn't have to. Of course, I did.

The light inside the taproom and restaurant was dim. As it was gray outside and the windows of the ancient building were but small, the electric light had been switched on above the tables. The latter had been cleaned only recently, as they still bore traces of wetness. The chairs had been placed on top of them, seats down, in order to make work easier for an elderly female who was mopping the wooden floor. The smell of detergent mixed unpleasantly with that of stale coffee and cold bacon fat. I saw Barb wrinkle her nose. The elderly woman vanished into the kitchen without a greeting as soon as she noticed us.

The bar in the back was dark and deserted. Barb steered me towards it, regardless. She made herself comfortable on one of the bar stools and indicated wordlessly that I should do the same. She placed her hands on the counter quite leisurely as if she were simply an ordinary customer. A few moments later, a barmaid emerged from the kitchen door and approached us from behind the bar.

"Hi there. Sorry, our breakfast hours are over, and we are not open for lunch yet. Maybe you want to return in about half an hour?" Her eyes were red-rimmed, and her sleeves were rolled up to the elbows. One of her forearms glistened with suds.

"We are looking for Rose," Barb said as if Rose were an acquaintance of hers.

The girl's scrutinized us warily. "She didn't show up this morning. I knew you couldn't trust a Roma. They are always here today and there tomorrow. Thanks to her I look like I do. Cutting onions, washing dishes. Not my job usually."

"Didn't show up?!" I repeated.

So, there must have been more to her upset last night than I had guessed. But, of course, in the light of her missing scarf, my earlier idea of her being connected to the body in some way became even more probable. Barb remained unperturbed. She reached into one of her coat pockets and drew out her badge.

"Detective Superintendent Barb Tope," she said, cool as a cucumber. "Could I talk to your boss, please?"

"He will also be in only in about half an hour."

"Well, maybe you can give him a call and tell him to come in a bit earlier. He might appreciate that our conversation won't be overheard by anybody else."

"Has Alan done anything wrong?" The girl's eyes became wide as saucers.

Barb stayed silent as a sphinx. The girl began fidgeting.

"Okay, okay ... I'll call him."

She went over to where the wall telephone hung and pressed a speed dial button. A second later, she was hectically mumbling words into the receiver which was trembling in her hand. She furtively looked at us every few moments while she was talking, shielding her mouth and the receiver with her other hand. Finally, she hung up.

"He'll be here in about five minutes. You're lucky he lives next door."

"See how much difference a phone call can make," Barb smiled blithely. I didn't miss the note of amusement in her voice.

The barmaid shrugged. "Can I get you anything to drink meanwhile?"

"A cup of coffee. Black. You, Emma?"

"Ginger ale would be nice, thank you."

We received our beverages just as Alan rushed in through the kitchen door. He must have entered the house through the backdoor that also served as the employee entrance. He looked pale this morning. There were dark rings under his eyes. He had a bad hair day, and he had botched his shaving job, as there were two cuts on his chin that he had covered with tiny scraps of tissue to stop their bleeding. He hastily removed them as he reached us. Then he gave me a nod.

"Emma."

I nodded back. Suddenly, I felt tongue-tied.

"Detective Superintendent Barb Tope. Sally told me over the phone you had some urgent business with me?" he turned to Barb, who took off her knitted hat, finally. He didn't smile and just waited for her to say something.

"I do," she stated and showed him her badge.

Alan didn't even gaze at it but looked surprised. "So, this is not about you being our house guest but all police business now!" he exclaimed.

"Let's call this a coincidence. I'm as surprised as you." Barb's voice sounded as cool as ever. "I never caught your name. You are Alan …?"

"McLeod. – You have come about Rose Buckland?"

Barb swayed her head. "What can you tell me about her?"

"Depends whether it's relevant," he evaded.

"Let *me* decide that. But let's start with her background. She is one of your kitchen helps, I'm told. Tell me more about her. What she is like. Where and how she lives."

Alan took a deep breath. "She's nineteen, single, lives with her father. She took the job when they moved here into their winter quarters about a good month ago." He squinted at Barb. "They are Roma, in case you need to know. She has been working here every winter season since she quit school at age sixteen. That's a typical thing for Romany girls to do."

"The kind of work or the school thing?" I asked curiously.

Alan threw me an angry look. "Don't know why that should be *your* business, Emma. Why are you here with her anyway?"

Before I could say anything, Barb stepped in. "That, Mr. McLeod, is *my* business. And maybe we stop discussing what's necessary to talk about or not, but get down to the facts. You might be glad to be done before your first patrons arrive. Just answer Emma's question, please. I' would like to know as well."

Alan hung his head. When he looked up again, his eyes had lost all fight. "Okay, Detective. So, yes, it's normal for Romany girls to leave school when they are sixteen. It keeps them away from the Gorja. That is the term for everybody who is sedentary and not a Roma. A lot of families want them to marry in their own closed circle. And until that happens, they live within their family boundaries. In Rose's case this is currently at Mr. Buckland winter quarter."

"You know him?"

Alan shook his head. Then he continued to describe the girl. "Rose is very tidy – another thing typical for the Roma."

"Is it?"

"Cleanliness is one of the fundamental musts for physical health. Which is really important if you are traveling a lot and under very limited conditions, at that. Think living space. Another reason why I like to employ Rose is her reliability."

"Until this morning?" Barb asked.

Alan bit his lips and didn't reply.

"When was the last time you saw Rose?"

Alan glanced at me. I almost choked. His gaze was fierce. I knew why. If I hadn't been around, he could have made up anything. But he knew that I had seen him and Rose last night. He, therefore, had to tell the truth whatever the consequences would be.

"Last night. Emma can confirm this. She saw Rose and me go into the kitchen."

"That's an interesting detail, though." Barb looked at me with a sardonic smile. "Why didn't you tell me?"

"I didn't think it was relevant," I claimed. "Besides, we didn't know until we got here that Rose hadn't shown up for work this morning."

"But it was no surprise to *you*, was it, Mr. McLeod?"

Alan harrumphed. "No. She ... she didn't feel well last night, and I agreed that she didn't have to show up for a while."

"For a while?! And was there a specific reason she didn't feel well?"

Alan sighed. "A rendezvous gone wrong."

Barb raised her eyebrows until they looked almost like circumflexes. "A rendezvous gone wrong," she repeated.

"The person she was supposed to meet didn't show up."

"Oh?"

Alan squirmed behind the bar. Then he grabbed a glass from a shelf, and tapped himself some water. He emptied the glass in a single gulp, then placed it on the counter in front of him.

"Why do I have a feeling that you know even more details, Mr. McLeod?"

He breathed in deeply. "When she came to the place where they were supposed to meet ... There was crime scene tape all over the place."

"Meaning where?"

"The towpath."

"When did she get there?"

"After she had finished with the first evening shift last night."

"And she started work when?"

"At ten in the morning. We have ten-hour shifts. With breaks to share a meal."

"So, she was here all the time?"

"From ten in the morning through eight at night, yes." Alan looked at Barb helplessly.

"Is there anybody else who can confirm this?"

"You can ask the entire kitchen staff."

It was me, now, who took a deep breath. So, Rose Buckland had an alibi for the time of the murder. If she had been expecting to meet the Roma who had been killed, it must have come as a shock to her to arrive at a crime scene instead. Did she even know that the guy had been killed? Or did she think that he had killed somebody? If they had been meant to meet at night, why had he been there early in the afternoon? And how come he had had Rose's scarf?

I looked at Barb. She was smiling at Alan.

"Thank you for your time, Mr. McLeod. If you happen to remember anything else, please, give me a call. I might not be in my room at all times."

She handed him a card. The pub door opened, and a group of construction workers spilled in from the cold outside.

"And just in time for your first lunch customers, too, I presume."

10

Barb and I split after the interview with Alan. There was no more to be said. We were stuck in a cul-de-sac with the investigation. And my first suspect, Rose, had already proven to have an alibi. Good for her.

We still didn't know who John Doe was. We *did* know that he had Rose's scarf – maybe the meeting had been about returning the scarf to her? But the more I pondered that, the less sense it made. He could simply have turned up at the pub and handed over the scarf. To Rose or any other employee, in fact. Instead, he had been waiting in the towpath. In the afternoon. But Rose had turned up only in the evening. Something was wrong with that. To find out what, I had to find Rose.

Barb hadn't asked where Mr. Buckland lived with his daughter. I had been too enmeshed in my own train of thought to ask for the address of his winter quarters. And I didn't want to go back to the pub – possibly running into Barb there – and to have to squeeze the info out of Alan. I'd have to use my own devices. Logical investigation.

If Mr. Buckland and his daughter, Rose, came to Ealingham-on-Ouse or its vicinity each and every winter, there was a probability that so did the people whose fires Ozzie and I had spotted the night of my arrival. I sighed. That meant I had to borrow Ozzie's truck, after all, and brave the English left-hand traffic. In a continental truck. Well, at least I was used to vehicles that had the steering wheel on the left and the gear shift to the right of the driver's seat. If it had been a British truck, I'd have sooner or later found myself in a ditch. Literally.

I walked back to Ozzie's home rather leisurely. There was no reason to hurry. The Romany or Irish Travelers – whoever the people were out there in the Fens between Mildenhall and Ealingham – wouldn't disappear into thin air all of a sudden. Unless, of course, they were connected to the murder in any manner. Which I thought, more or less, unlikely. Of course, one never knew, and I'd have to be very careful how I went about asking them about Rose.

Back at *The Heron*, I went into the kitchen where Ozzie kept all his keys in a drawer. I rummaged through it until I found the one for the truck. To my surprise I realized that my fingers were trembling. The thought of driving in Britain for the first time had me made all jittery.

I looked into the mirror before leaving the house again. I wanted to look okay but not overly so. I wanted to impress the people I was going to pay a visit favorably. That meant I couldn't arrive there like a fancy big-city girl. I wanted to get information. I had to seem approachable.

I stared at Ozzie's vehicle. I had never driven a truck before. Only my little yolk-yellow beetle and two other used cars before that. I hoped it wouldn't be too difficult. I had watched Ozzie drive a lot; so, the only difference seemed to be the parking brake that was under the dashboard.

I climbed into the driver's seat and adjusted its settings and that of all the mirrors. Then I took a deep breath and started the motor. How would I get to the other side of the brook that was flowing between that winter quarter and the main road we had come by? I had only a vague idea about junctions that didn't look much like leading anywhere.

Once I was on Main Street, my nervosity rose. Driving in Britain, driving to a place I didn't know to people whom I didn't know with a mission of which Ozzie would not approve – to say the least – was certainly not what I had planned to do when I came here. Yet, here I was.

Traffic was low. Ealingham soon lay behind me, and the green-beige marshes of the Fens with plowed fields in between glided by. Square church spires looming out of a woodsy knoll on the horizon indicated there was another small town or village. Fat pigs moved in the muddy grounds of a farm closer by the road, and I held my breath as I drove through the particular smell. I couldn't imagine a more rural and remote landscape that was yet so close to big cities than this. You could get lost, for all I knew.

Actually, I found the winter abode I was looking for pretty quickly. It was another story to get there, though. Several times I thought I'd made it, only to have to turn around in the very sight of what looked like a trailer park with a utility building at one side. Finally, I found the narrow turnoff between hedges and a drystone wall that landed me at my destination. A group of children had assembled at the end of the country road. They were pointing at me, giggling and nudging each other, apparently because of my multiple failed attempts to reach their settlement.

Their clothing was poorly, colorful, and mismatched. But the small faces looked full and their bodies well nourished. There were a few dogs chained to the trailers. Several wrinkled faces stared at me through the windows. I felt like an intruder already. And not one who was welcome, at that. I slowly got out of the truck and held on to the door, waiting for somebody to permit me access to the site.

After a while, a woman about my age pushed her way through the crowd of kids. She wore a dress way too thin for this kind of weather and held a crocheted triangular scarf clutched over her chest. Her distrustful eyes were focused on me all the while. At one point she flinched and reached to one of her feet – her shoe had come off in a spot of mud, and she had to retrieve it. Which caused more giggles with the children. Finally, she stood, arms akimbo, about three yards away from me.

"So, you've finally found the right turnoff, huh?" she mocked me. "Must be pretty urgent business you have with us that you are so insistent on getting here."

I wasn't sure whether she meant this as a statement or an invitation to tell her about my purpose. I decided to interpret it as the latter.

"I was wondering whether you would be able to tell me about one of yours," I began.

She tilted her head, and her brown eyes glinted with quiet amusement. "One of ours. Nice way to express yourself." I felt heat rise in my face. "So, you mean a traveler? A Romany person in general? Or one from our group here?"

"I meant somebody who is a Roma ..." My voice faltered.

"You know how many there are in this world, don't you? I know a few but not all of them." I heard someone snicker behind the doorway of a ginormous trailer with a canopy. Other women were showing their faces, interested on what was going on. I guess my arrival meant a change to their tough everyday life. Sort of a comic relief.

"I have come about Rose. Rose Buckland."

"She's not one of ours."

"You mean she doesn't live here?"

"No, she certainly doesn't." The woman turned around as if she considered the conversation ended.

"Would you be able to tell me where I could find her? Please?"

The woman just turned her face over her shoulder. Her long tresses moved like thick strands of silk. In an odd way, she looked mysterious and attractive.

"This time of day she'd be at the pub in Ealingham. She's working for somebody else instead of her family."

I didn't understand what she meant. To me, earning money and probably contributing it to the household budget *was* working for one's family. But I decided not to ask her to explain her view. Instead, I continued, "And if she isn't there – where does she live?"

The woman eyed me, swept around, and came another step closer. "You probably already know that she lives with her father?" I nodded. "The other side of Ealingham. In an old farmhouse. The road has no name. The house has no number. Still, you can't miss it with that piece of garbage of theirs next to it."

"Piece of garbage?" I was totally clueless.

"A vintage caravan from the 1940s," the woman spat. "You Gorja don't know a thing about caravans, fine people as you are, do you?"

I shrank. No, she was right. I had seen lots of caravans and RVs at a big annual show in Stuttgart, even climbed inside a few. But they had all been brand-new. And as I was not really into this kind of lifestyle, I hadn't taken the trouble to remember brands or model names.

"So, how do I identify this caravan?" I asked meekly.

"Oh, trust me, you will know her when you see her. She looks like a modern version of every cliché you've ever known about vardos." She laughed. My mouth fell open. "*Vardo* is another one for you. That's a traditional Romany wagon like our women in the fortune telling business usually have."

"Thank you."

"Why do you want to see Rose anyhow?" She put a foot forward and suddenly was the incarnation of Bizet's Carmen, thin dress, muddy shoes, and triangle scarf included.

"I found a scarf she has lost," I said. It wasn't a lie. I didn't have to tell the woman, though, that I wasn't in possession of the item. Nor that the scarf had been held very firmly by a male hand. The hand of a dead man. A dead Roma without a name yet. I didn't know how much they already knew about the murder on the towpath. But it was surely *not* my business to be the messenger of that news. Besides, I didn't even know whether that man had belonged to their group.

The woman's face became mellower. "Lost her scarf, huh?" She drew hers more closely around her now shivering body. "Be careful when you go there," she said in a softer tone. "Her old man is not exactly the kind you want to deal with."

"Is he dangerous?"

Another hoarse laugh. "One never knows with men, does one? But his temper is vicious enough that he keeps to himself. There are no other Romany people who want to live in a group with him." She gave me a wave and started to leave. When she had almost reached the trailers again, she looked at me one last time. "He inherited the caravan and a gun from his father – and his anger. All from World War II. They have never liked our kind. But the way his family was dealt with caused him scars that are worse than those other English Roma bear."

I watched her climb the steps to the trailer from which she had emerged earlier. She closed the door behind her. The children came towards me now, trying to figure whether they could coax any candy out of me. I had none, and I cursed myself inwardly that I hadn't thought of children being around in the first place. Next time – if there was a next time – I'd make sure I brought something for the kids.

Finally, I got behind the wheel of Ozzie's pick-up again and drove away from the site. The circle of trailers grew smaller in the back mirror and vanished behind the bushes and trees that grew by the brook. When I crossed the bridge and reentered the main road, I felt as if I had left behind a different world.

11

I went back to Ozzie's home and grabbed an apple and a yogurt for lunch. I was not much of a lunch eater, my favorite meal being dinner. And, every once in a while, a delicious and abominably rich English breakfast with my love. I just didn't feel like the latter when he was not around.

Then I switched on Ozzie's computer. He had told me his password before he left, so I had access to whatever I wanted to look into. In this case, it was the vicinity of Ealingham. I wasn't keen on another awkward approach to a destination such as I had just performed at the Romany trailer park. Maybe, I'd find Mr. Buckland's house if I'd spot the vintage caravan from above. Unless, of course, the Google camera team had passed by during summer when the Bucklands had been on the road with it.

I was lucky. After a few times of zooming in and out on single houses in the Fens on the other side of Ealingham – there were more of them on the satellite picture than I had anticipated– I found something that looked like a strange shape next to a building. I was able to drop the orange Google mannikin onto the main road, though not next to the house, and to make out what looked like the modern version of a vardo, painted green and white. I took a deep breath, zoomed out again, and changed to the less bewildering map grid to figure out which turnoff to take. When I had found it, I simply printed out the map. Then I slipped into my coat and woolen hat and drove off again, this time into the other direction.

What would I say to Mr. Buckland? Would he even talk to me? Or would he threaten me with this gun I had been told about before I was even able to introduce myself? All kinds of scenarios popped up in my mind, none of them promising. I had to stop fantasizing and simply concentrate on my next step. On finding the turnoff.

Ealingham lay behind me once more, and I actually enjoyed the November dreariness of the lonely Fen landscape. There were drains and canals that wove their ways through the meadows and fields. Some crows were stalking solemnly around a puddle in an empty paddock, probably looking for what the usual inhabitants had left over of their feed. I passed a bicyclist, then a tractor. And that's when I missed my turnoff because the tractor had blocked my view. I thumped my right fist on the wheel. Now I'd have to turn around somewhere.

As there were no other junctions, I had to drive into the village that I had spotted on the horizon. When I made a U-turn through the gas station at its entrance, a black cat ran in front of my car and I had to brake hard not to hit it. It had come out of nowhere from the left and vanished to the right as quickly as it had appeared. Now, I'm not superstitious by nature. But this incident made everything seem even more auspicious. Though I wasn't even sure whether the direction of the kitty's journey would mean good or bad luck.

I drove back about a mile and, this time, found the turnoff immediately. The road was narrow, and I was glad that there was but this single house at the end of it. The probability of any other car approaching and me having to back up was almost zero. Still, my nerves were on edge, and I felt my throat tighten as I neared what I presumed was the Bucklands' home.

It was a two-story brick building with white window frames, a white front door, and chimneys at each gable end. It was sitting above one of the wider canals, with a dock but no boat in sight. There were curtains in the windows, and an old but lovingly polished gray Mercedes sat on a gravel patch on the side of the house. I decided to turn the truck around in case I had to leave in a hurry, and parked it next to the car. When I got out, I realized that my knees felt a bit weak.

I still had to verify that I was at the right house. So, I passed its front quickly to look for the vintage caravan. And indeed, there it was on the other side – a gorgeous piece of history. Not at all the piece of garbage the Romany woman had described. She had been right about the modern version of a vardo though. I walked up to a side window and stood tiptoes to peek inside.

"What are you doing here?"

I whipped around, my heart beating in my throat, blood rushing to my head, all my limbs going weak, and my tummy turning nauseous. Stupid, stupid me! Of course, I would have been watched as I approached, the appearance of a visitor neither invited nor announced. And to pass by the front door and disappear from sight ... The man I was facing had all the right to be furious at me and my curiosity.

"I saw this from the main road. This is beautiful," I tried to placate him and pointed at the caravan. Of course, it didn't work.

"What are you doing on my property?"

"I ... I..."

The man was short and wiry. His black hair was thinning, but his brownish skin was almost unwrinkled. It was hard to estimate his age. He could easily be anything from my late thirties to a decade or two older. He wore a tidily ironed shirt and black pants – dressed as if to go out. His dark eyes were sparking anger and defiance, and his full lips were pressed together tightly as he was taking me in. He didn't hold a gun to my relief. He had folded his arms over his chest, every bit in charge of the situation. And he was waiting for my explanation.

"I'm sorry," I finally got out. "I just wanted to verify that I'm at the right home, and I knew that this gorgeous vintage caravan had to be my means of identification." Oh my, did I really talk this stilted?!

"Well, and peering inside was helpful?" he asked cynically.

"No. No, of course not. I just couldn't resist."

"You don't belong here."

"I know. I'm sorry. May I have a new and better start to introduce myself? Please?"

"I meant you aren't English. You sound German to me."

"I am. Emma Schwarz." I blithely offered him my hand. He ignored it.

"And what brings you here, Fräulein or Frau Schwarz? A German intruding on a Romany home. Not that this is such a historically new situation, is it?"

It hadn't occurred to me earlier, and I could have slapped myself. The burden worse than that of other Roma about which the Romany woman had talked earlier in the day could only mean one thing. Mr. Buckland's family or at least part of it had fallen victim to the abysmal persecution and extinction of their ethnic minority that my people had committed against them during the Third Reich. His ancestors wouldn't just have been discriminated; some of them might have been brutally murdered. And here I stood, a German, sticking my nose not only into his family business but also pressing it against part of his private property, one of the caravan's windows.

"I assume you are Mr. Buckland? I'm looking for your daughter, Rose."

"What do you want of her?"

"She might be missing a scarf, and I know where it has ended up."

Mr. Buckland's laugh sounded bitter. "I should hope she didn't lose more than her scarf."

I didn't understand what he meant and must have looked it. Mr. Buckland shook his head, his face the picture of frustration.

"I wouldn't know what you are implying."

"So, you know Rose?"

"I don't. I have only seen her at *The Bird in the Bush*, and I know that she works there as a kitchen help."

"Well, those days are counted, for sure," he grumbled more to himself.

"You are moving out again?"

"*She* is. Because she is going to marry one of ours just as she ought to have years ago. Any good Romany girl marries and founds a family as soon as they are out of school. But not Rose. Oh no! She thought herself to be better than that. But I found her out. Spotted some of her school books under her mattress and made sure that she couldn't learn from them anymore. Burned them to ashes. Studying for graduation in secret! As if she were meant for a different life. But I won't have that!"

"But Rose is of age, isn't she?"

Mr. Buckland seemed to remember my presence again. "Yes, that's the Gorja idiocy they teach at schools. And that's why we pull our girls out before their mind gets too bent and they want to turn their back on our traditions. Of age! If she were married already and had a bunch of kids tied to her apron strings, she'd have enough on her hands and wouldn't think rebellion."

"But education doesn't hurt anybody."

"Doesn't it?! *You* probably had as high an education as they can get back where you're coming from. Are *you* married? Do *you* have children?" I stayed silent. "See?! See?!"

I didn't know what to answer. So, he was worried that Rose would break the Romany family pattern and choose a different path. And in saying he hoped that she hadn't lost more than her scarf, he was implying that she might have lost or taken off more clothing or even lost her virginity in order to defy her heritage. In short, he suspected that she had made love to somebody he didn't know or didn't approve of. A Gorja.

"So, you are trying to make her marry somebody before she changes her life?"

"The marriage is already agreed on," Mr. Buckland stated, sounding grimly satisfied.

"By her?"

"What's it to you? She will succumb to our traditions. Now get out of here."

"But about her scarf ..."

"She's not here."

"But ..."

"You just heard. Rose didn't come home last night. She isn't in the house. She isn't in the caravan."

"But then, where *is* she?!"

"You're saying you saw her at the pub? That's where she works. That's where she encounters Gorja men. Go back to the pub and ask for her there. *They* will know."

"But she didn't show up for work today!"

Mr. Buckland stared at me, bewildered. "She didn't show up?!"

"No. That's why I assumed that she was at home. With you."

"Well, she's not." He clammed up. "Go now."

I nodded. "Thank you, Mr. Buckland."

He didn't say a word but stepped aside to signal I was to walk past him. I did. I strode towards the truck. Not too fast – Mr. Buckland didn't scare me. Not too slow – I didn't want to annoy him more than I obviously already had. When I opened the truck door, he was standing by his front door. Our eyes locked once more. He broke the connection and stepped inside. I dropped into the driver's seat and exhaled. This hadn't gone entirely wrong. But not exactly right either.

12

I almost forgot to pick up Rocky for his usual afternoon walk. So, when I finally turned up at Henry's door, he just squinted at me, said something unintelligible, and shuffled back into the hallway. I heard him call Rocky, and the black Labrador rushed to the door, leash between his flews. The musical theme of a TV quiz show started in one of the rooms and floated to the front door. Henry returned, gave me a short nod, and closed the door. I had made him miss the first moments of his program, and he had made it clear that he didn't approve of my tardiness. I sighed, put Rocky on the leash, and strolled towards the dike and the towpath by the river Ouse.

The rest of the afternoon was uneventful. The crime site tape had been removed, and I encountered some joggers who came from the other direction, their faces determined. I brought Rocky back after an hour. Then I waited for Ozzie's call. I let him do all the talking and simply didn't mention where I had been today. He would have been quite upset with me. If I had been him, I would have felt the same way.

So, I listened to him describing the bazaar he had visited a few hours ago. He told me he had bought some gifts for me. And he raved about the food he had found in a tiny restaurant off the beat to which he would take his airmen for dinner – if they were willing to taste the real deal of Moroccan cuisine, not the burgers and touristy kabobs they were serving at the pool bar of their hotel.

Ozzie sounded happy and relaxed, and nothing could have made me happier, either. When he hung up, I felt that wave of bliss rush through me that he had become such a part of my life.

When dinner time came, I decided I'd head over to the pub again. First of all, I wasn't comfortable in this large, empty house at the back of the dike anymore. It was way too close to the crime site, and there were too few neighbors around. Second, I didn't want to fall behind as to what was developing in the case. The closer I was to the people involved, the more possible it was that I'd catch hold of another clue or two. The people involved being Detective Superintendent Barb Tope and publican Alan McLeod. I wasn't sure what I expected to happen. But I wasn't going to let it happen without me. I had already witnessed too much to back out without any further attempt at getting to the bottom of the story.

So, I walked through the dimly-lit streets of Ealingham. Somebody had decorated their front yard with an illuminated and inflated Charlie Brown, an inflated Snoopy, and with a life-size Santa that was climbing part of their home's façade. I wasn't sure how much influence American culture had over here, especially in the surroundings of an American air base. I knew that there had been Guy Fawkes Night only recently, with bonfires and all the associated traditional trappings. Ozzie had told me that Americans living off-base got their share of candy-begging trick-or-treaters on Halloween in the area, too, but that those who celebrated rarely ventured into the countryside. It was mostly a matter of convenience to stay on the main thoroughfares in the bigger towns, parents driving their kids from place to place, guarding their well-being while quietly speculating how much free candy they would be able to wheedle from their kids for their services later. So, now it was all about Christmas already, and instead of Charles Dickens characters, the Peanuts had made it into this front yard.

It was a clear, cold evening, and the stars were twinkling above. The moon was but a waning sliver in a seemingly endless black sea. All the more did I enjoy the sight of the pub's windows with their golden glow and the sound of laughter and conversations that came through the heavy wooden door even before I pushed it open.

Inside, it was toasty, and the air smelled of pies, fish and chips, and spilled beer. In one corner of the room, a group of men and women hung out around a target. The thumping of darts hitting it mingled with the clicking sounds from the pool table next to them and with the clinking of glasses. Alan's voice called orders into the kitchen. Yesterday night's barmaid pushed herself through the crowd at the side of the bar, carrying food to one of the tables. My mouth was watering.

I squeezed myself through to the bar and caught Alan's attention. He smiled at me. But this smile looked strained, and it didn't reach his eyes. He came over.

"Emma, how are you tonight?"

"Quite fine, thanks. You?"

"Alive and kicking," he said, but I heard the double entendre and knew that by now he must have heard about the body by the towpath. "Cider?"

"Please. And I'll also have a look at the menu."

He grabbed one from underneath the counter and handed it over to me. Then he walked over to the taps, and I could watch the bubbly citrus-colored brew stream into a fresh glass. A moment later, he pushed it over to me.

"I'll have the two-piece haddock and chips basket, please. And a Knickerbocker Glory for dessert."

He raised his brows but accepted my order of an ice cream and meringue sundae on a cold November night anyway. "You eating at the bar or at one of the tables?"

"I'll find myself a table, thank you."

I pushed myself off the bar and threaded myself through the crowd. It seemed like last night's table was again not taken. So, I sat down there and spent the next ten minutes observing the customers and the barmaids. Every once in a while, the headlights of passing cars cast their beams through the window. Barb was nowhere to be seen. I was almost disappointed.

A barmaid came to my table with my basket of food and the usual condiments, malt vinegar and ketchup.

"Need anything else?" she asked.

"Has Rose shown up today?"

"Rose who?"

"Rose Buckland."

"The kitchen help? No, as a matter of fact." She seemed surprised. "Now that you say it! What about her anyhow?"

"Oh, I just wanted to chat with her about a scarf she may have lost. And it has been found."

The barmaid's face clouded over and she bent slightly forward. "There are rumors that they found a body over on the other side of the dike. On the towpath by the river," she half-whispered urgently. "They say he's one of those gypsies. But nobody knows for sure. Rose is also one of them. Do you think this is why she hasn't shown up?"

I shook my head. "Sorry, I have no idea what you're talking about," I claimed. "It was just about the scarf and that she wasn't in this morning. So, I simply tried again."

The barmaid shrugged and straightened up. Then she said in her normal voice, "Nah, don't know where she is. To be honest, I don't know much about her. She's not much of a talker. During her breaks she usually sits with a book and studies. School books. At her age!" She giggled. "Enjoy your food!"

I looked at my basket. Two big pieces of glistening, steaming, deep-fried fish and a humungous pile of fries – unfortunately the thick-cut variety that always seemed to stay limp and soggy, no matter how long they were fried. I doused the fries with malt vinegar and dug in. It tasted quite good, and the tiny bowl of cucumber salad that they had added to the basket rounded out my meal pleasantly. When I was done, the barmaid returned, took my empty dishes, and delivered my colorful dessert five minutes later. I had to admit, service was great and quick at Alan McLeod's pub.

"Oh my, if it weren't too cold, I'd order one of these, too!"

I looked up from my tall glass, full spoon almost at my lips.

"Barb," I grinned. "Why was I just thinking it would be nice to have you sit down and pay me company?!"

Barb smiled back sardonically. "Is it because you like my company as a person or because you'd like to hear how my case is going? I'm not supposed to tell you details, you know." She pulled out a chair and let herself fall into it. She was looking tired, and her nose was slightly red. "Do you think they have anything against an oncoming cold?"

"Ask them for a glass of hot water, a spoonful of sugar, and a shot of rum," I suggested. "If it doesn't help, at least you don't feel the cold that much after a sip or two. Old German sailors' remedy."

"But you are living in Filderlingen near Stuttgart, don't you?"

"Ah, but I spent my childhood and youth in Hamburg."

"Was your dad a sailor?"

"No, but my Aunt Maria, who raised me, swore by such remedies. Just not for us kids," I winked.

"She better not," she replied with a slight sparkle in her eyes. "I'll give it a try."

She looked around for the barmaid and was soon able to place her order.

"You still don't have any grilled cheese sandwich, do you?" she asked, and the barmaid denied, as she had done last night. "Well, and I guess you won't make an exception and create one for me, would you?"

"Sorry," the barmaid said. "Ploughman's Lunch or …"

"… mac 'n' cheese, I know. I'll take that with extra cheese, please. I need something to warm my bones tonight." Barb rubbed her hands, and the barmaid headed for the kitchen. "You wouldn't know what a circus it was to get a rental today. First, I had to wait for a cab for ages. Seems like there are hardly any available when you need them. Then, the rent-a-car place would open only later, and I had to wait for a full hour. I hadn't seen this coming and walked around, of course. If I'd known about the wait beforehand, I would have dressed warmer."

A glass of piping hot water was placed in front of Barb along with a shot glass of rum and a sachet of sugar. As Barb mixed the components, a bittersweet fragrance wafted over and reminded me of dreary childhood days when Aunt Maria had laid down to soothe her cold with a grog, as she called the brew, and usually ended up groggy after a double shot in hers. I still wondered whether the term "groggy" was derived from abuse of the beverage.

"So, you got yourself a car, though?" I asked with fake cheer to make the false nostalgia go away.

"Did," Barb said and tried the first sip. "Not bad. – Well, and then I drove over to Cambridge to check back with the crime lab and with pathology. Of course, *that* had to be in a chilly basement room, all tiles and coolers. I guess that was where I got the final blow."

"I doubt it," I replied. "A proper cold takes three days in coming, will stay three days, and takes three more days to disappear."

"Let me guess – your Aunt Maria?"

"The same."

"She still alive?"

"Very much so. But we were never close."

"It happens."

The mac 'n' cheese arrived, a giant helping decorated with sprigs of parsley and also a tiny bowl of cucumber salad, not on the plate but in a separate bowl next to it. Barb's eyes lit up, and a few moments of utter silence ensued as she speared the first bites of floppy elbow noodles and gooey strings of cheese. I finished my sundae and gave the long spoon an extra-lick. Then I counted to twenty to give Barb a bit more time before I restarted the conversation.

"Why the trip to the pathology anyway? I mean, it was obvious how the poor man was killed, right?"

Barb swallowed. "Sure. Shot. But what caliber? Therefore, what kind of gun can we exclude from the investigation?"

"But the case I found …"

"Is no proof at all until the size of the wound and the effects on the body match up with the size of the case and – even better – with the bullet. Now, the DNA on the bullet has to match that of the victim."

"You found one this morning. Was it the one you were looking for?"

"They couldn't tell me yet," Barb sighed. "Our DNA lab is totally backlogged with analyses. But with some luck, I might get the results in a couple of days."

"And meanwhile, the killer is running around, possibly looking for further victims. "I was aghast.

"Possibly but not likely." I looked at Barb, questions unspoken. "We rarely have to deal with serial killers."

"So, once the DNA on the bullet has been cleared or whatever you call that …?"

"Then we'll check for the marks on the bullet that were inevitably caused by its travel through the barrel. These marks are pretty much like a fingerprint."

"And then you still have to find the gun," I pondered remembering my discussion with Ozzie. Had it really only been yesterday?! "And even if you do, it's not clear whether the owner of the gun or another person was the killer."

Barb had laid her fork onto the table, wrapped both hands around her glass, and taken another sip. Now she scrutinized me. "You are quite informed about stuff like this. For somebody who mostly reviews cultural events and does surveys on topics of the more peaceful kind, I mean."

"You're forgetting who is my friend these days."

"Oh yes, Master Sergeant Wilde. *Oscar* Wilde." Barb chuckled. I felt my feathers ruffled. "Sorry. But names like these are too rare not to cause a reaction. And yes, I went on base, too, to talk to your friend's commander and get to know the regulations for privately imported arms into Great Britain. So, you can put your worries to rest about any Americans from base involved in this respect. But it could still have been anybody."

"Quite discouraging," I sighed.

"Quite. But not hopeless. I'll simply have to follow the bullet. So, in a couple of days, we should be making big progress." Had she said *we*? "Sergeant Cameron, Constable Williams, and I." She looked at me with a smile that was the tiniest bit sardonic. "You didn't think that this included you, did you?"

"No."

"There you go." She retrieved her fork from the table and continued enjoying her pasta dish. She pushed away the cucumber salad, though. "Not my kind of dressing," she explained between bites. "I don't like sweet vinaigrettes."

Alan was making his way over to us. He exchanged some friendly words to the left and to the right as he was doing so, which took him longer than he must have intended. His eyes looked haunted. Finally, he reached our table.

"Everything alright for you ladies?" he asked. I had a hunch he was after something else than a compliment for the kitchen.

"Absolutely," I confirmed.

"Say, is there a bit of Gruyère in this dish?" Barb asked.

Alan nodded. "You got some fine tastebuds, Detective."

"Some hunches, too. You didn't come from behind the bar to ask how we like our food. You didn't come and ask yesterday night ..."

Alan's shoulders slumped. "That obvious, huh? Well, I was just wondering what impact the towpath thing could have on business in our village."

Barbara squinted her eyes at him. "Try better. You want to know how deep we are into the investigation already. And why is that of any interest to you?"

"Well, the killer could still be around ..."

"True. But any killer involved in any case could be." Then she relented. "Tell me about gun ownership around here. Who is known to be a hunter? What hunting estates are there around? What shooting ranges? Are there any gun afficionados such as in collectors? You could help me immensely if you made me a list of people and places where I could begin my search."

Alan sighed. "I'm not sure I know that many of either."

"But as the publican, you encounter a lot of people who talk about their quarry, don't you? Or hunting outings?" She tilted her head slyly.

Alan blushed. "I could give it a try."

"You could," Barb grinned. "And I might have a dessert yet. Maybe another of these grogs and a baked apple."

Alan, knowing that he had been dismissed with no information whatsoever but with a task on top of it, turned around frustrated and went back to work.

"Do I look like an information office?" Barb asked nobody in particular and shook her head. "I'm here to gather facts, not to distribute them."

I bit my tongue. She let on about more she knew than she should if one handled her right – which I presume I did. I just wondered whether she would also give me access to Alan's list. Somehow, I knew I'd have to be faster than her to obtain it. Again.

13

I held out until Barb called it a night. After her second grog, she announced that she felt drowsy and intended to sleep in the next morning to cure her cold. The lab results were expected only in two days anyhow – she would simply take it easy tomorrow. She looked like she could use a good dose of tight sleep, for sure, when she left after having settled her bill.

I should have felt tired, too, after such a long and eventful day. But I was wired. There was too much to find out. Where was Rose? Who was John Doe? Who had shot him and why? How were Rose and John Doe connected? What did Alan know? Because I had not even just a hunch that he knew more than he let on. I was dead sure.

As the night before, I walked up to the bar and found myself a tiny corner to squeeze in between the wall and a rough looking farmer. He barely glanced at me, nodded a gruff greeting, and that was it. I wasn't unhappy about it. The less attention I got, the better.

But Alan saw me settle in at the bar, of course, and he didn't look happy about it, at all. I knew that if he could have avoided serving me and enduring my company, he would have done so. As it was, he just raised his brows in question from the other end of the bar, and I mouthed, "Cider, please."

"Pint?" he asked.

I nodded, and he grabbed a fresh glass to tap my drink. When he came over to place it in front of me, I managed to get hold of his elbow.

"Alan, is there any chance I could talk to you? Please?"

"Now? You can see well enough how crowded it is. This is not a good time to talk, at all."

"Then, what *is* a good time?"

"You don't want *her* to sit in on this. Is that it?" I knew he meant Barb and nodded. Alan relented. "I'll have a short break in about an hour – I always do, right after dinner service ends, two hours before last orders. Come over to the other side of the bar then, and I'll take you into the back."

I released Alan's elbow. "Thank you."

He barely acknowledged me for the rest of the time, and I was on tenterhooks about what he might be able to reveal. He had taken care of Rose immediately last night. He had looked worse for the wear this morning whatever had been going on the night before. And he had tried to pry information from Barb about the murder on the towpath. Why?

Finally, the clock over the bar showed that it was only two more minutes till Alan's break, and I slipped out of my corner which was immediately occupied by another customer. I walked to the other end of the bar and leisurely leaned against the wall, trying to be inconspicuous. Meanwhile, the barmaid who had worked the tables so far, got behind the bar and took over for Alan.

I gazed over to the tables. There were still guests, but all of them were only concerned with their beverages.

"Follow me," I heard Alan's voice by my side. He whipped his head in the direction of the kitchen, and I quickly stumbled after him.

The kitchen behind the bar was fairly big. Bigger somehow than I had imagined. I watched the chefs box up food and clean their stoves. A busboy was hosing off the dirty dishes and piling them into an industrial dishwasher. A kitchen help had begun wiping off all of the prepping surfaces. Alan waved me towards the back entrance, a metal door next to a huge walk-in cooler. He grabbed a coat from a hook before he opened the door for me. I stepped outside. An automatic light flashed on and lighted the back alley. We stood between a number of restaurant dumpsters. Not a very inviting environment. I tentatively looked up to the windows upstairs.

"No worries, she can't hear you. Her room goes out to the front." Alan was standing next to me now and lit a cigarette. He drew on it, inhaled deeply, and then let out a long cloud of bitter smoke. "What kind of a game are you playing anyhow, Emma? You pretending to be her friend while doing your own thing?"

I looked at him, miffed. "I'm not pretending. I really like her."

He shrugged. "Kind of convenient, though, isn't it? – So, what do you want of *me*?"

I swallowed hard. "That list you are going to make for Barb – could I have a copy? Please?"

He laughed bitterly. "Ozzie will kill me if I do."

"He won't get to know."

Alan sighed. "Emma, I hardly know you. But this is not a place you should put yourself in. There has already been a death. You don't want to risk being in the killer's way, do you?"

I huffed. "I'm already in way over my head."

"What? How so?"

"It was I who found the body."

Alan gasped. "Oh, for heaven's sake. That's awful!" His face went ashen, and he gagged. Then he took two swift draws on his cigarette, tossed it to the ground, and stomped it out. He buried his face in both of his hands for a moment. Then he looked at me. "Can you ... can you describe him?"

"How do you know it wasn't a woman?"

"Trust me, there is no woman other than Rose involved in this. And you already know that she didn't do this."

"How can you be so sure?"

"Because there are only few options, and they are all male. Now, can you please describe him?"

"Will you tell me what this is all about, please?"

Alan took me by the shoulders. "Emma, this is really important. Can you ..." He had grabbed me so hard that I winced. He cussed under his breath and released me.

"He was young. Apparently, he was a Roma. And he held a scarf in his hands."

Alan nodded and slumped against one of the dumpsters. He stared to the ground with unseeing eyes.

"Alan?" I rubbed my shoulders and tried to get his attention in waving my hand in front of his face. "Hey? You okay?"

He shook his head as if waking from a dream and took me in with dazed eyes. The he turned around to walk back inside again. But I was quicker and gripped him by the arm.

"I told you everything. Now it's your turn. What do you know about this?"

Alan's eyes were streaming when he looked at me again. He stifled a sob. Then he wiped his face. "He should have been waiting for Rose."

"I know. I mean, that's what I figured. Can you start from the beginning, please? When Rose came into your pub last night, what had happened?"

Alan sat down on the doorstep. He pulled another cigarette from a crumpled package with trembling hands and lit it. He inhaled deeply, exhaled. Silence. Then, "Rose was to meet somebody to take her away from here. From her father's plans for an arranged marriage. She wanted to determine her own way of life. So, this was somebody who would have brought her to a safe place until she'd have married her real love. That was it."

"That's not *it*," I insisted. "There is much more to the story. Let me recapitulate. Rose is in love with somebody but is supposed to marry her father's choice. So, she tries to run away with the help of somebody in order to marry her sweetheart. How did she know that guy?"

"That guy?"

"The John Doe who was killed."

"John Doe …" Alan laughed mirthlessly. "No, she didn't know him. Her scarf was a way for her to recognize that it was he who was to help her escape."

"How was he able to get her scarf when she didn't even know him?" Alan stayed silent. "Wait! You?!"

Alan cleared his throat. "I'm part of an organization who helps the women of Irish travelers and Roma to get their rights. There are quite a few around here during winter. And we are used to see a lot. Children who are sick, breaking into our homes and businesses to steal. Women who look beaten. Men who are in need of work to support their families. They are on the fringe of society, and though there is some kind of awareness for them, it's never enough. They have never been integrated because they have a different way of life. And because of that, they get marginalized. People are suspicious of them. And a thieving child or a beaten woman is not the best way to create trust in people who are so different. Especially the Romany people here."

"So, you belong to an organization that knows people who help others to escape from their way of life?"

Alan hung his head. "He had begun living like a Gorja himself back in the day."

"You talking John Doe now?"

Alan nodded. "It wasn't easy for him. The color of his skin, his foreign features always betrayed his different heritage. They say that clothes make the man – it's only true to a degree. Anyhow, he was happier away from his old life. At least that is what he said. And he wanted to help others to achieve this happiness, too."

"Was there any money involved?"

"As in a human smuggler?"

"Yes."

Alan shook his head. "He had a regular job and did this without any profit for himself." His eyes brimmed over again. "He was a good guy."

"What was his name?"

"Is it important? He's dead anyhow."

"It might help us find the killer."

"Trust me, it won't. Nobody even knew he was around."

"Except you, Rose, and said killer," I pointed out.

"Codona," Alan whispered. "His name was Patrick Codona."

"So, you told Rose she needed to hand you a token of recognition, and she handed you her scarf?" Alan nodded. "And she was supposed to meet him on the towpath. But when she got there, it was already a crime site taped off, and Codona's body had been removed. So, she came back here."

"She thought that somebody might have attacked him, they had killed him, and then run away."

"Great," I said and paced in a circle. "Just fantastic. So, where is she now? You probably know that she is not at her father's home. Do you have your hand in hiding her, again?"

Alan looked to the ground, took a last draw from his cigarette, tossed it, and trod on it. Then he looked up at me with blank eyes. "I have no idea. I called another number of another guy from our organization. Within an hour, Rose was picked up and taken away."

"And I am to believe this? That you don't know where she is, I mean." I stared at him grimly.

"It's better nobody knows," he replied quietly. "The less known, the less told." He rose. "Got to go back inside again. You coming, too?"

I shook my head. I needed to take a walk and wrap my head around the story I had heard just now. The walk home – that is, to Ozzie's home – would provide me with the undisturbed silence and inspiring motion that I needed to make sense of it all.

Alan stretched his limbs and wiped his face one more time. Then he opened the backdoor. I gave him a tiny wave as he disappeared inside the doorway and carefully sought my way over the slippery, mossy cobbled back alley till I reached the lights of Main Street again.

14

The next morning, I felt a slight scratching in my throat as soon as I woke up. My right ear was aching, and that was the surest sign that I had a cold coming. Great! I didn't care where I'd caught it – I simply wanted it gone. I rummaged in what medications I had stowed away in my closet and found a few sachets of Lemsip. I was relieved – at least I could do something against the worst effects immediately.

I took my time enjoying breakfast – toast, marmalade, a soft-boiled egg, two rashers, and the Lemsip – and watching some rabbits hopping through the soggy backyard. The bushes were dripping wet, their branches hanging heavily over the empty garden beds that Ozzie and I had planted with potatoes, onions, tomatoes, and cucumbers in early summer and harvested during my past visit. Now, everything that was left of our effort was the blackish-brown soil that we had carefully turned and fertilized with compost for next year. The radio was playing smooth jazz interrupted by traffic news and concert announcements, every once in a while. And the washer next to the stove was running a load of my clothes and a few of Ozzie's.

In the middle of it all, the phone rang, and I got up to fetch it from its place in the hallway.

"Hello?"

"Oh good, you're still alive!" It was Linda.

I had to laugh. "What did you expect?! I'm vacationing."

"Well, the last I heard from our friend Niko was that a British detective superintendent whose name I forgot was checking your identity because you had found a body. And that has been – let me see ... pretty much 48 hours ago. Knowing you and your awful curiosity, by now you have interviewed at least two people who are either suspects or could lead you to the killer. And you are probably planning your next steps right now." Linda simply knew me too well. I grimaced. "And you don't like it that I know this."

"I was just enjoying my breakfast," I tried to soothe her.

"Eating has never stopped anybody from thinking," Linda claimed. "By the way, do I hear something nasal in your voice?"

"Got a cold coming on."

"See?! You better stay inside the house and tend to yourself. Chicken soup made from scratch should help a lot."

"I don't have any chicken in the house."

"That's a lame excuse for not staying at home."

"Is not," I protested and thought that I sounded a bit like a nine-year-old. "Besides you should carry a cold into the fresh air."

"Your Aunt Maria?"

"Spot-on."

"Well, as I can't keep you from doing what you've got your mind set on, I might as well try my bit to save you from harm."

"As in?"

"Run by me what you've found out."

"It's not your case, Linda, remember?"

"Not yours, either. Even less so – you are not a policewoman."

"But a journalist." I took a sip of my medicine. "Okay, I'll humor you." And I began to tell Linda the story of Rose's arranged wedding that she tried to evade by running away to a safe place and there to get married to her lover.

"Isn't this arranged marriage thing a bit old-fashioned? And this getting a girl out of school at sixteen, too?"

"I know," I wailed. "Horrible, right? As far as I know, there are Civil Rights movements and other organizations that the Romany have founded in Britain. And they are set to provide equal education and health services to traveling kids, to modernize their life-style, to try to further integration and acceptance, and so on, and so forth. But what can you do if you have a father like Mr. Buckland?!"

"Do you know who Rose's lover is?"

"No, I don't know his identity, yet. I'm sure I'll figure it out sooner or later."

"This publican, Alan, probably knows it," Linda interjected.

"Probably. It slipped my mind last night because it didn't really seem that important."

"Not that important?! He is a piece of the puzzle!"

"I know. But everything was so upsetting. The fact that Alan has a hand in this. Seeing him cry. And that seemed to be genuine grief, mind you."

"Right."

"Anyway, Rose's contact was shot in the afternoon. Remember – I think I heard the shot, not a car engine backfiring. But she was to meet this Codona guy in the evening, after dark. Now, I'm totally bewildered why he was already there in the afternoon. Pretty much six hours before he was expected."

"With the scarf?"

It dawned on me. "You think that he was lured to be there early?"

"Nothing else would make sense," Linda remarked dryly. "He must have thought it was Rose who asked him to be there earlier. But obviously it wasn't her – she's got that watertight alibi."

"So, whoever lured him there must have known of the arrangement …"

"Seems like it, doesn't it? Think it over. You can do that at home. Promise to try?"

I sighed. She sighed. She knew I wouldn't, couldn't just stay at home.

Click.

There I sat, almost choking on my toast. Of course – how could I have overlooked that possibility that somebody had found out about Rose's plan?! The question was just who and how? And what interest had the killer in shooting Codona? And what else did Alan know that I hadn't asked him about? About what had he, maybe, simply decided to stay silent?

I felt antsy, but I had to finish some household chores. I wanted to give Ozzie's home as much love as I could, so he would return to a nest that was clean and cozy. Also, I wanted him to return to some prepared food in the freezer that he'd just have to defrost and reheat. So he wouldn't have to cook as soon as he came home. He usually took his own food on base, as the chow hall was on the other side of the runway, quite a drive from where he worked in his office. With some culinary provisions made by me, he'd have time to relax when he returned from his mission. Of course, I'd have preferred it way more if we could have done all of this together. But I knew that as a military sweetheart I'd always come only second to duty.

Time flew, and it was close to noon when I finally had a few containers filled with fragrantly steaming food. The lids were still off, so everything could cool off. And I had labeled the lids. Ozzie should be able to recognize at first sight what was in which container when taking one from the freezer.

What would I do for lunch? I decided I'd walk over to *The Bird in the Bush*. With a bit of luck, I'd be able to have a chat with Alan. Hopefully, Barb was out and about, though. Or still laid up. I didn't have the intention of getting caught digging around in her case.

It was drizzly outside, and I put on the sturdiest shoes I had brought here. They completed my rustic outfit. Nobody cared about elegance in the countryside anyhow. Not when it didn't involve social events. I grabbed one of Ozzie's umbrellas from the umbrella stand and stepped outside. There were puddles in the driveway, and the dike looked forbidding in the gray daylight. I wished the river would have been in plain sight. That would have made it so much more picturesque. Just like Mr. Buckland's house. But one couldn't have it all. And what Mr. Buckland's home had in location advantages, it lacked in other aspects that I deemed more important. I wouldn't have wanted to swap homes, after all.

I deeply breathed in the fresh air. It smelled of wet stones, rotting foliage, and dung. Somebody must have fertilized their nearby fields. Smoke rose from some chimneys – not everybody had central heating like Ozzie had at his home. The road was deserted, so was the one that led up to Main Street. I avoided the puddles on the sidewalk as well as I could, but the spray of passing cars on the thoroughfare rendered my effort to stay dry useless. I felt pretty disheveled and uncomfortable when I finally entered the pub.

The room was nearly empty. An elderly couple was just about finished with their early lunch, and a worker in overalls sat at the bar, having a beer and eating fries with his fingers, daintily extending his pinky. A young woman was polishing glasses and cutlery at a sideboard next to the bar. Alan was nowhere to be seen. I sat down at a table close to the bar, so whoever was going to serve me wouldn't have to walk all across the room.

"Hello Emma," Alan said. He had appeared as out of nowhere. He must have been busy in his tiny office that also served as the reception area for the few rooms upstairs. He seemed even more fatigued than yesterday, most certainly due to our conversation last night. Also, he didn't look pleased to encounter me again. "What can I do for you?"

"Toad in the hole and a Sprite, no ice, please," I said.

He nodded and left for the kitchen. A few moments later, the young woman came over with a glass of Sprite. Alan made it clear that he wasn't keen on my patronship today. Still, he wasn't able to avoid it entirely because, ten minutes later, he returned with a plate filled with my order. The sausage was pretty much neglectable in flavor, but the Yorkshire pudding around it was all it should be, and the onion gravy tasted heavenly. I sighed with pleasure. Alan, meanwhile, was back in his office.

When I was finished, I settled my tab at the bar. The worker had left a while ago. So had the couple. I sauntered over to Alan's little office nook, entered with a light knock, and posted myself right across from him. Alan looked up, irritated.

"Emma, please, let the entire story rest. I just don't want to talk about it anymore."

"But you are thinking about it, too, very obviously. You look as if you hadn't slept well last night."

He folded his hands on the tabletop. "What do you expect? A man that I called was killed because of that call."

"But why? And by whom?"

"Trust me, if I knew why, I'd know by whom. As it is, it might as well have to do with his past as with Rose's future. Who knows? Besides that's what the detective superintendent's job is. And you better keep it at that."

I sucked in my lower lip. "Just give me one last information – who *is* Rose's sweetheart?"

Alan sighed and drove his hands through his short hair, then crossed them behind his head. "You're not one to give up easily, are you?"

"Giving up too soon means missing out on the full story," I countered.

He let his hands sink. "Michael Thornton."

"A Gorja," I stated.

"Not a Romany man, if that is what you mean."

"Precisely." I frowned. "Does he live in the area?"

"You said, *one* question."

"Come on," I tried to coax him.

"Balmer Hall," he gave in and rose. His answer took me totally by surprise. I was about to open my mouth, but Alan quickly shut me down. "Enough now. That is all I know. And if you have to, you can figure out the rest." He was already passing me to go back into the taproom.

I nodded. "Thank you." I followed him. "And I promise you …"

"Don't." Alan whirled around. "Just don't. I just want my peace of mind."

I lifted my arms apologetically.

At that moment the pub door opened, and a young man came in. One whose face I remembered immediately. And I had no doubt at all who he was. It was that young man who had picked up the envelope that night I had been here with Ozzie. To be honest, if his clothing had been less leisurely elegant and expensive, I might not have recognized him. And I certainly wouldn't have found him familiar at all in a different setting. He looked pretty inconspicuous. Just a nice, fresh young man's face, cleanly shaven, a businesslike haircut to his brown hair, slim, somewhat athletic, average height. No outstanding features, at all. But here he was, at the pub, and he would have stood out even if there had been a crowd. Which was how he had caught my attention that last pub night with Ozzie.

As I was curious what he came about, I kept myself to the background and made myself as invisible as possible by slipping to the side of the bar. As Alan concentrated on the man, I slid behind the counter and hunkered down below it. Quite inconvenient, but it was the best place to eavesdrop under the circumstances, for certain.

"Michael!" I heard Alan exclaim. "I thought you were to meet Rose …"

"Alan …" I imagined they were shaking hands. "I was. But she isn't where she was supposed to be. What happened?"

I heard how wood scratched on wood – presumably by moving chairs –, and I imagined that the two men were sitting down. Probably across from each other. I held my breath.

"I heard there was a murder on the towpath where Rose was supposed to have been met. I am besides myself. Is Rose …?"

"Rose is safe. It was the person who ought to have met her and brought her to the safehouse."

"Who was it?"

"Does the name matter?"

Pause. Then a quiet, "I guess, no."

"Patrick Codona was his name. Ring any bell?"

"No."

The silence stretched. So, this was Rose's lover. From Balmer Hall. All of a sudden, I envisaged the young man to be our former tour guide's son. Would that gentleman approve of his offspring's choices?

"Well, if Rose never met him, where is she now? Did she go back to her father?"

"She didn't. As soon as she returned here, all upset, I made another phone call, and somebody else picked her up. We didn't know whether the safehouse was safe anymore or had also been compromised, since the person whom she was to meet in secret was found out and even killed, as we know now. I expect to get a call soon to be told where she is. For now, just assume that Rose is safe."

"I ... I ... I just don't get it. Why would anybody do this? Why can't Rose go away from home as any normal grown-up? Why do there have to be all these precautions to get her out just to set her free and let her live her life like anybody else?"

"I have no answer to these questions, my friend. Except that it is harder for some Romany people than for others to choose a different way of life. Some need help from outsiders. That's where these precautions come in. It's a different culture that you simply have to accept."

"I *do* accept it. But can't we *all* just interact on a more open-minded level? And where does murder come into this? I mean, this is sick."

"It is. – Since you didn't know Codona, it makes no sense asking whether anyone from *his* past could have killed him. Based on events that weren't even connected to Rose's escape."

"I have no idea," the young man replied after a short pause. "But it seems more logic that the killer knew that Codona was to meet Rose and then caught him out."

"It does. But it makes no sense that Codona turned up so early."

So, Alan had come to the same conclusion as I. That was somewhat reassuring. That also meant that Barb would probably be on the same trail, as well. I wasn't sure I was happy about this.

At that moment, I heard the pub door squeal and some heavy steps stop shortly after entering.

"And where are you two hiding Rose?" Mr. Buckland's voice yelled.

15

"Don't!" Alan's voice was suddenly trembling.

The young woman who had been polishing glasses and cutlery at the sideboard before, suddenly rushed behind the bar and past me to vanish into the kitchen. I only heard the backdoor clank shut.

"Geez!" Michael exclaimed.

"Where is my daughter?"

"She isn't here. I swear, man," Alan said. He sounded panicky, and I was wondering in my little hideout behind the bar what was going on. It sounded frightening. I let myself down on all fours, praying that I would be able to move noiselessly. I crawled to the end of the bar, peeked around the corner, and froze.

Mr. Buckland was standing with his feet widely apart, his eyes blood-shot, wielding a gun. Alan and Michael had both jumped up. Alan was white as a sheet; so was Michael. I could hardly believe my eyes. This looked like a scene from an Italo-Western movie, and usually that foreboded bloodshed. I tasted iron on my tongue, and my tummy flip-flopped. Yet, I managed to stay quiet.

"Listen," Michael said. "I know you don't like me. But Rose loves me, and I love her."

"Quiet!"

"Mr. Buckland," Alan ventured. "This boy here …"

At this moment, Mr. Buckland pulled the trigger. A shot rang out, followed by a "Ping" – probably the case hitting the ground – and by the dull thud of a bullet impact with something solid. My ears protested with a tinnitus-like sound overlaying everything around. I was deafened for a moment. Then, I heard a muffled scream, and I saw Michael grabbing his right sleeve with his left hand. Blood was squelching through his fingers and started dripping down on the wooden floor of the pub. His mouth shaped a wailing O.

Alan had jumped sideways, but Mr. Buckland now aimed the gun at him. It was a gun with a wooden stock and comparatively little metal. It looked pretty heavy, but Mr. Buckland didn't seem to mind the weight. He waved it to signal Alan to move over to Michael's side. Alan complied; he was staggering as he did so.

"Now, you tell me where my daughter is." Mr. Buckland stared at Alan. "She was last seen in here. That means you must know where she went."

I had managed to creep back behind the bar. I was shaking. With trembling fingers, I pulled my phone out of my coat pocket. Luckily, Barb had made me save her number in its contact file. Luckily, I remembered right now. I had never thought I'd ever dial her. But now, I preferred that very much to the rather anonymous emergency number that might end me up just anywhere. I messaged her.

"Help! Gunman at Ealingham pub. One wounded."

I waited, praying to get an answer from Barb. But there was none. Meanwhile, Alan talked a mile a minute to save his life, while Michael was only squirming and making small animal-like noises. If Mr. Buckland had thought he'd get any information out of the latter, he had gotten it all wrong. Michael must be in such shock and pain that he was unable to say anything coherent. And Alan made sure to keep things common place and to soothe Mr. Buckland as he would have a drunken customer ready to pull a barfight. Which it was, kind of, only way worse.

"Don't give me this bull!" Mr. Buckland suddenly yelled.

I held my ears just in time for the second shot that I sensed was coming. A number of bottles on a shelf above me burst, shedding glass and liquid all over the place. My hair got sprayed with a load of rum, whiskey, and tiny glass shards.

"If you continue to talk like a psychiatrist, I'll shoot up your entire bar. Where is Rose?"

Pause.

"Where is ..."

"I don't know, man. Honest to God," Alan whimpered.

I had no clue what was going on. I didn't even feel safe behind the bar anymore if Mr. Buckland was to follow through with his threat. I might have tried to creep into the kitchen and flee through the backdoor. On the other hand, here I was, a witness.

"So, you tell me that you have seen Rose leave. And that was it. Only, why didn't you call when she didn't turn up the next morning? Because you knew her whereabouts. So, either you are hiding her or you know where she went. Right?"

The menace and fury in Mr. Buckland's voice sent goosebumps over my back. It didn't help that my coat was soaked through with liquor.

"I told her not to return the next day," Alan claimed. "She had not felt well at all after finishing work."

I didn't know that he had it in him to weave such a story in such a situation. For a moment, his voice wasn't even wavering. That was probably because part of the story was true. Rose had been more than upset at finding the crime scene. And Alan had known that she would not return to work … What a presence of mind!

"So, you claim there was a mutual understanding that she wouldn't turn up for work?"

"That's exactly what I was saying, Sir."

"And you …"

I didn't dare move anymore. I knew that I would hurt myself leaving my current position to watch the scene that was about to unfold. Besides, my weight would cause the glass bits to be ground into the floor – which meant noise. I surely didn't intend to be the third person staring at the end of a barrel this noon. Where, for heaven's sake, was Barb? Why did it take her so long?

Just in the nick of time I realized that I still had the sound for notifications switched on. I managed to press all the right buttons to mute them, fingers feeling like they weren't mine. The moment I had done so, a window popped up.

"Coming."

I stifled a sigh of relief. I waited.

"You are a damned Gorja who is trying to take away my daughter from her family. Just to steal her innocence. And the next thing you know is you'll drop her like a hot potato to have fun with one of your own. Because that's all your kind are thinking of. You lack family values. You ditch all of your traditions and cultural values. And then you aim to destroy that of others."

Michael sucked in air through his teeth. He didn't give any answer.

"You point with fingers at my people. You gossip about us. You shun us. You libel us as lazy, treacherous, dirty, violent."

Well, at least the last rang like the truth in my ears. Mr. Buckland *was* violent. But I also heard the pain in his accusation. I wasn't sure whether I wanted to understand what he was saying. That would have meant empathy. And you couldn't have empathy with somebody who was brutalizing other people just because *he* felt in pain.

"Please, Mr. Buckland, could Michael sit down?" Alan tried to convince the enraged Roma.

Apparently, there was a silent affirmation for I heard the legs of a chair scrape on the floor.

"Thank you," Michael managed to say.

"Mr. Buckland, Sir." Alan made use of the miniscule pause. "May I say that both sides obviously are fighting prejudices? And in this case, we are dealing pretty much with a Romeo and Juliet story. These two young people of two very opinionated families love each other. Michael here would never do wrong by Rose."

"And how would you know this, McLeod?" Mr. Buckland spat. "Have you read into his soul? Do you really know whether his family's sordid ways haven't grown roots in this Gorja's heart as well?"

"Have *your* stern ways taken root in Rose's?"

"A woman is supposed to obey her guardians – and the first is her father."

I could have puked. This was so old-fashioned and from the times when women still relied on a man paying for her needs. These days, any girl could get an adequate education – which was what Rose seemed to be yearning for – and make her own living. Which, of course, took away a lot of importance from the male role. Independence didn't sit well with anybody who took their self-esteem from a social structure that built on dependences and suppression.

Fortunately, neither Alan nor Michael had to reply. For at that very moment, the pub door burst open.

"Hands up! Drop the gun to the floor!"

It was Sergeant Cameron's voice. He sounded triumphant. I guess it had been his dream to be able to say these words just once in his life. Now, shortly before likely retirement, this dream came true. A dream that every kid who wanted to join the police probably had. I would have given a fortune to have seen his face. Well, maybe not a fortune.

Then, there were steps from the side entrance that also led up to the guestrooms.

"Escape is useless," Barb said calmly. "Drop the gud, Mister." My, her cold was really bad!

I heard a muttered cuss and a heavy object hit the floor. I was poised for Mr. Buckland to yet try and make a run. But the fight might have left him. I heard the clicking of metal – handcuffs, was my guess.

"You do dot have to say adythid, but it may harm your defedse if you do dot metiod whed questioded somethid which you later rely od id court," Barb quoted. Sounded like an English version of the Miranda Rights I knew so well from U.S. movies. I'd never thought I'd ever hear similar. Nor in such a terribly nasal way. If the situation hadn't been so serious, I'd have burst into laughter.

On the other hand, the thought of her ordeal brought my own snivels on again. And suddenly there was this wild itching urge in my nostrils.

"Where is Emma Schwarz, by the way?" Barb asked.

I rose from my hideout. Glass fell off me, and my wet coat clung in new places as I straightened my body.

"Achoo," I sneezed. "Achoo, achoo!"

16

Detective Superintendent Barb Tope squinted at me without a smile. "Of course, always in the thick of things."

"Guilty, your honor," I tried to joke. "It's not always on purpose, though."

Barb didn't even smile, then. She just walked over to Michael and took a look at his wound, endangering her mauve sweater to be soiled with the young man's blood.

"Emma!" Alan exclaimed. "You're still here?!"

"What the hell is *she* doing here?!" Mr. Buckland grumbled.

"It was her message that saved you all from greater trouble," Barb explained. "Anyhow," she was turning to Constable Williams now, "call in the medics. Tell them it's serious but not life-threatening. No lights and sirens necessary."

Constable Williams went outside to make the call. I shook out what glass shards I still had in my hair and tried to sneak past Barb to escape further scrutiny. I was out of luck. Her hand held me back by my coat sleeve.

"You are going nowhere, I'm afraid," Barb said. She sounded a lot different when she acted the detective she was.

I shrugged. "Where do you want me in this family picture?"

Barb looked around the room. "Sergeant, could we have a couple more chairs at this table, please?" Unceremoniously, she led Mr. Buckland to the table at which Michael and Alan had been sitting before, and gently urged him to sit.

"Mr. McLeod, Emma, you, Mister What's-your-name …"

We all followed suit, also Michael, who started to shake from shock under a space blanket that Sergeant Cameron had laid around his shoulders.

Barb looked into each of our faces. "What a motley group of people, I say. Now, Mr. McLeod, you are the publican, of course. Still, you seem to have interesting connections that are out of the ordinary, hm?" Her eyes went back to the shooting victim. "You? Who are you?"

"Thornton, Ma'am. Michael Thornton."

"You're lucky that the bullet didn't hit you. Just some splinter from that beam. But why did Mr. Buckland shoot, at all?"

"You better ask *him* that," he gnashed his teeth.

"I want to hear it from you, for now."

"He thinks I know where his daughter, Rose, is. He thinks I'm hiding her."

"Are you?"

"No."

"What is your business here this noon?"

"I came here to ask Alan the same." He swallowed. "Where he is hiding Rose, I mean."

"Alan?!"

"Mr. McLeod."

"Say, Mr. McLeod, I knew you might be an interesting figure in here. So, in the chain of suspects about the disappearance of Rose Buckland you keep coming up as the end of the chain. Which puts you at the center of interest. Isn't that so, Mr. Buckland? Why, then, did you shoot at Mr. Thornton?"

Mr. Buckland squirmed in his chair. He must be uncomfortable with his hands fettered behind his back.

"That bastard is the reason for all of this!" He nodded at Michael.

"All of what?"

"May I?" I interjected. "Seems it's a love story against family wishes. Capulets? Montagues?"

Barb laughed mirthlessly. "I didn't expect *you* to put it in a nutshell. – Mr. Buckland, is Frau Schwarz here right? Is this about a love affair that you oppose?"

Mr. Buckland looked even grimmer, his dark eyes sparking fire. If he could, he'd have probably jumped up and slapped me.

"Mr. Buckland?" Barb insisted.

"He's a Gorja. He wants to turn my daughter into one as well."

"Is that so, Mr. Thornton?"

Michael looked almost as if he were about to swoon. "She has always been more one of us then of them."

Barb sighed. "Great! So, what is this all about? A shoot-out because a young woman is in love and you don't like the lover?" She rose and walked over to where the gun still lay on the floor. "Looks like an antique to me. M-1 Garand? Where did you get this, Mr. Buckland?"

"It's been handed down in my family," Mr. Buckland said, pride in his voice. "My great-grandfather fought in Normandy, along with the Americans."

Barb's eyebrows shot up. "You mean World War II?"

"Yes, Ma'am."

"But your family is of Romany descent?"

"Yes, Ma'am."

"How come he brought home a U.S. rifle?"

"That's a long story of no further importance," Mr. Buckland said, and his face turned blank.

"I've got time," Barb said coolly. "And I decide what is of importance. You brought along this gun and shot at somebody with it, after all. Let us have the story. All of it."

"Does *she* have to sit in on this?" Mr. Buckland pointed at me with his chin.

"I know it is inconvenient for you. But as I don't want Frau Schwarz to wander off on one of her sleuthing excursions and due to a shortage of personnel, I have to keep her here for the time being. No worries, she won't talk about this to anybody. Right, Emma?" She gazed at me fiercely. I just nodded. "There you go. So, tell me, why would your Romany great-grandfather join in the Battle of Normandy?"

Mr. Buckland sighed. His eyes took on a far-away look into a world only he was able to see.

"My great-grandfather had family in Germany. We were a big clan with branches all over Europe. Of course, he heard what was going on there way before anybody would believe him. The deportations and concentration camps. They said these were unproven rumors. He dreamed of helping to free our family out of the concentration camp in which he thought they had been imprisoned. There had been a general conscription here in Britain, as we all know. So, he was serving in the military already. When the opportunity came to actually fight on the continent, my great-grandfather asked to be transferred. I have no idea to which places he went after surviving the first days in Normandy. I know that he followed his orders although he was treated vilely by his Captain. When the war was over, he brought home this gun. Said he swapped it with a G.I. friend of his. He never found or brought home any of our family."

The room had turned silent. I only heard the humming of the bar fridge. There were no sounds from the kitchen – apparently everybody had disappeared through the backdoor as soon as Mr. Buckland had entered with the gun. Good for them. Alan interchanged a look with Barb, and she nodded. He rose, walked over to bar, tapped some soft drinks, and returned with glasses for everybody.

"Please continue, Mr. Buckland. So, the origin of the gun was never proven," Barb encouraged the man.

He breathed in deeply. "Could I, please, have one hand freed to drink?"

"A straw, please," Barb turned to Alan. Then back to Mr. Buckland, "Sorry, but not possible under the circumstances." Alan brought a straw from the bar, and Barb helped Mr. Buckland to his drink. Meanwhile, some medics had arrived. They bustled around Michael, mostly silent, with only the scantest comments to each other. I saw Michael wince a couple of times but wasn't able to see what they did to his arm.

"My great-grandfather married a Roma and had eight children with her. My grandfather, his oldest son, inherited the gun. My family returned to the traditional Romany civilian way of life. Then, my father received the gun as a wedding gift from my grandfather. He and my mother were a fiery couple – lots of love, lots of violence. The cliché I saw made me wish I were different. Especially, when I went to school during the winter months. With all the Gorja children. I thought there must be a way out. There was. I managed to get decent grades in school and to graduate at the top of my class. Against my father's wishes, I didn't marry but enlisted in the army. I was deployed abroad. I was proud to fight. The only drawback was the Captain I served with. Same family as that who bullied my great-grandfather. You see, the commanders liked to keep people from the same place together, assuming that they fought better when they were neighbors. Only, they didn't reckon that not all neighbors are friendly with each other. I had thought I could become a Gorja and be accepted as one in taking up arms against a national foe. I found myself betrayed. When I came back home after a couple of turns, I married a Gorja girl I had courted during my leave. She betrayed me, too, but left me with Rose. That's when I returned to our traditional ways. That's why I was set that no Gorja will ever hurt Rose like they have hurt me and my family. I want to keep her safe. And the only way to do so is to keep her under my eyes and to give her in marriage to a sound Romany man."

Mr. Buckland fell silent. Nobody spoke. After a while, Mr. Buckland turned his head to Michael who was bandaged by now.

"Want to know where the men came from who bullied my great-grandfather and me?"

"Where?" Barb asked softly.

"Balmer Hall."

Mr. Buckland's eyes were hard as pebbles. Barb looked clueless.

Alan heaved a sigh. "They were Thorntons," he explained with a helpless look at Barb.

"Does your daughter know?"

Mr. Buckland's laugh was bitter. "Have you ever tried to reason with somebody in love?"

"So, you brought a gun because that was better than reasoning?"

Mr. Buckland hung his head and shook it.

"You are aware that this was premeditated and might get you into big trouble?"

He nodded.

"Were you aware what role your family plays in Mr. Buckland's denial to your marriage to Rose?" Barb looked at Michael now.

Michael shook his head. "I had no idea. My father never talks about the war. I always thought it had something to do with PTSD. He never even mentioned he knew Mr. Buckland. He just told me never to marry beneath my station, whatever that means in a modern society in which the importance of aristocracy is more than debatable and everybody gets a chance to move upward. We're only untitled, landed gentry, for heaven's sake!"

Barb took a long sip from her glass. When she set it down, the medics quickly shook hands and exchanged business cards with her.

"Email is fine," Barb said. "Just in case I need you for more medical info." Then she turned to Mr. Buckland. "An M-1 Garand shoots what kind of caliber, Mr. Buckland?"

I wondered. She knew exactly. And yet she asked Rose's father. To what purpose?

"30-06 centerfire."

"M-hm." Barb got up from her chair and searched the floor with her eyes. Then she stepped towards another table, bent down, and picked something up with a Ziplock bag. She seemed to carry a secret stash of those with her. Then, she returned to the table and showed the object to Mr. Buckland. "This came from your gun, Mr. Buckland?"

He nodded.

"What do you know about the murder on the towpath day before yesterday?"

Mr. Buckland's head snapped up, and his gape left no doubt that it was the first time he heard about it. "A murder? Where?"

"Here in Ealingham."

"Who was killed?"

"One of your own, Mr. Buckland."

"What was his name?"

My eyes flew to Alan who sat stiff as a rod in his chair and seemed to have a hard time to breathe.

"We don't know the name yet. We are still running our data base of fingerprints again his."

I couldn't keep quiet any longer. "His name was Patrick Codona."

"And how do *you* know?!"

"I told her," Alan said quietly.

Barb's head flew around, her eyes locking with his. "You owe me a long explanation later. – Mr. Buckland, did you know Patrick Codona?"

Rose's father shook his head. "Never heard that name in my life."

17

After this, a long afternoon unfolded. Mr. Buckland was taken into custody and driven away – I had no idea whether to Ely, Mildenhall, or even farther away. His case seemed clear – armed assault in two cases. Not even talking the damage he had done to the bar.

Michael Thornton was dismissed for now. His wound didn't keep him from getting into his car. He had been lucky. A direct hit with the bullet would probably have cost him his entire arm at that short distance.

Alan called his staff back into the pub to clean up and serve the guests as usual. They were probably shaken, as well. Only one of them showed up in the taproom to get their orders from Alan. After that, Barb and the policemen walked Alan and me over to the police station for further questioning.

We were seated in different rooms to tell our story separately. Barb threw me a look that told me I would get it yet after she was done with Alan whom she intended to put through the wringer. I pretended not to care. But I was glad to realize that I was done with my narrative way sooner than Alan was with his. After signing the report, I slipped out of the police station into the early dusk and walked home as fast as possible. *The Heron* seemed like a haven after the day's events. And I was pondering what I had feared more, being hit by the bullet or being reprimanded by Detective Superintendent Barb Tope for being in a place I shouldn't have been. Even though I hadn't known it would become a place of danger.

I felt ravenous once I reached Ozzie's house, and I raided the cupboards for all kinds of snacks, not discerning whether they were salty or sweet. I needed to eat. I didn't feel like cooking. Not even like reheating one of the dinners I had made for Ozzie. Chewing, I paced the kitchen. What to do now? And what kind of a strange story was unrolling in front of my eyes?

Generations of animosity between a Romany family and local landed gentry. The story of Cain and Abel all over again, of the settlers against the nomads, of distrust and prejudice.

Balmer Hall.

"Of course, back in the day, we didn't mince matters, and poachers were shot on the spot."

The memory flashed through my mind. The armory with all of these hunting rifles. Now, I wished I had paid more attention to the explanations, maybe even asked some questions. Such as what kind of ammunition these guns shot. Were they for birdshot only? Or were they for bigger game?

If the latter, could any of them have been used as the gun in the towpath murder? Where was Rose? Did she know about her lover having been wounded? About her father's arrest?

I walked over to the living room and switched on the old-fashioned TV set that had come with the house. There were only four channels, all BBC. I checked my watch. A few more minutes to the first evening news.

The phone rang. I frowned. Somehow, my bad conscience suggested it might be Barb. I didn't want to talk to her right now. Still, what if Ozzie … That thought decided it. I rushed to the phone and grabbed the receiver.

"Hello?"

"Sweetie, how often do I have to tell you not to run in the house?" I sighed with relief. "No, don't sigh. You know that this is the way accidents happen."

"I know."

"So, everything is fine here. We are flying somewhere south tonight because one of our planes there had an accident."

"Oh my! Bad?"

"Let's say the other guy looks worse. Collision of a delivery truck with a wing tip."

"I see a truck split open like a can."

"Probably. Anyhow, I might not be able to call you as easily from there as from here. Is everything okay?"

"Fine," I said quickly.

"Why do I sense you are in trouble?"

"I don't know. I'm not." I didn't even blush. First off, I didn't need him to worry about things he couldn't change. Second, it was not I who was in trouble but some people who happened to be around me. I didn't have to tell him that I was trying to help. He'd immediately tell me to stop it and think safety for myself first.

The upbeat beeping of the BBC news sounded from the living room. Ozzie must have heard it, too.

"Anything new on the towpath murder?" he asked.

"Oh my, how do you know?"

"We receive BBC news down here as well." I moaned. "So, it was a Roma, they say?"

"M-hm. But they don't know why he was shot. Could be anything."

"Well, you better stay close to the village, I guess."

"You know, I don't think the murderer will show up there again," I said lightly. "He has found his victim and has moved on."

"He?"

"Or she," I conceded. "Whoever did this."

"Well, you may be right. Still be careful, okay?"

"Okay."

"I love you."

"I love you, too."

We hung up, and I went back to check the screen. They were still covering foreign news. Elections in a South American nation. A visit of the Prime Minister at a convention in Paris. Violent protests against the government in Hong Kong. Then came inner politics. And finally, what I had been waiting for.

"There are new developments in the brutal, execution-style murder that happened a couple of days ago near the village of Ealingham-on-Ouse in Suffolk. Police state that the victim was identified as 29-year-old Roma Patrick Codona, who was known to belong to a Romany Civil Rights group aiding young women to break away from abusive families and relationships. As yet, it is not known whether such might have been the motif behind the assassination." The film sequence was showing the towpath, the crime scene tape, and Barb being interviewed by a TV crew. When had *they* come in?! Then the cameras focused on the solemn speaker's face again. "Police released photos of an item whose owner hasn't yet been identified." There was a picture of the colorful scarf, and I was bewildered. They knew it was Rose Buckland's scarf. What were they trying to do? "If you know the owner or her whereabouts, please call your local police station."

That was it. I switched the TV off again. What did they try to do? Did they want Rose to come out of hiding?

I paced. If Rose watched the news, whom would she contact? I tried to put myself into her shoes. There were only two possibilities – Alan or Michael. My instinct told me that she'd turn to her lover rather than her boss. She needed emotional support, and as much as I had seen Alan take care of her, I couldn't imagine him to be the first go-to person she'd choose for a heart-to-heart.

I checked my watch. It was almost seven by now. Driving over to Balmer Hall wasn't a good idea this time of night. Dinner time. I'd make a show of myself, and I wanted subtle. Also, Michael would have to explain why he was wounded. His family would be upset; they didn't need a stranger in their midst right now. Even if I didn't feel much sympathy for Michael's father or his forefathers after everything Mr. Buckland had told us, I sensed that the Thorntons' family bonds were at work now. Maybe, I could go over on a more inconspicuous level.

Ozzie's computer might hold the solution, I decided. Squeezing myself behind his desk, I typed in his password and googled "Balmer Hall". The site popped up immediately. "Balmer Hall – Tradition with Flair" a banner on top of the page read. Underneath, a constant loop of photos showed the building as seen from the main gate, the colorful kitchen garden (a picture taken in summer, obviously), the park with deer chewing the cud under the canopy of some ancient oaks and beeches, a wedding couple on the outside staircase, a hunting party in traditional gear in the courtyard, a buffet set in the dining hall, a picture of a row of old coaches, the wall of rifles, and the Thorntons' coat of arms. I scanned the options of further access into the site and chose "event calendar".

November held a few hunting parties for waterfowl in the area. There also was one for deer in the north later in the month, but I discarded the thought immediately. I had to check myself into something that was coming up as soon as possible. And here. I wanted to see the armory once more as well. So, why not connect a visit with Michael or another guided tour through the estate? Though I yawned at the thought of a second lengthy discourse about the history and importance of the Thornton family in Suffolk and beyond. It would have been different if an outsider had come up with an evaluation. But Mr. Thornton basically related his own family's biography somewhat with a tinge of self-adulation.

I was lucky. There were gun classes for beginners at the estate the very next morning. There were even two more slots available. I decided against registering online. They might not see it in time anyhow. I would simply show up; they wouldn't make a scene in not letting me join in front of the entire group, would they?

A tiny roil in my stomach rebuked me, though. This would be anything but inconspicuous. But it couldn't be helped. It was the easiest way to get back into the armory and maybe even to attain access to Michael without any further a-do.

18

The next morning dawned bright and chilly. The sky was a shade of blue that almost hurt the eye with its intensity. The lawn in the backyard was white with frost, and the branches of the bushes and trees looked prickly with icy particles. A bunny was hopping through the front yard when I left *The Heron* to drive over to Balmer Hall to participate in the gun class.

I had to scratch the truck windows clear; inside it was so frosty that it hurt to breathe. The vapor of my breath almost froze immediately to the windshield. I started the motor and cranked up the heat until I was able to see through again. Then, I went off on my investigation's next chapter.

As soon as I had left Ealingham, I was overwhelmed by the beauty of the frozen Fens. The marshes were glittering, and a soft vapor hovered over them, not yet ready to decide whether to fall and freeze or to evaporate in the bright sunlight. Smoke rose straight up from the chimneys of farmhouses by the road. It was quiet outside with hardly any traffic.

I passed through a neighboring hamlet a few miles away. A gas station and mail box were all that they had in public services there. I wondered how they would help themselves if they ever got snowed in. But maybe they knew in advance and were used to the isolation in such a case. People had to have a special disposition to live under such circumstances *and* to be at ease.

Then came the junction with the tree boulevard leading up to Balmer Hall. I remembered it from Ozzie's and my excursion. Had it been only a week ago?! I turned in and drove the half-mile or so up to the iron gate that stood invitingly open. The parking lot was filled with a number of cars already. I spotted two gardeners tending to hedges at one side of the large brick manor.

Balmer Hall was a typical country seat of the Elizabethan times. Its wings were half-timbered. There were gables galore, and a square turret overlooked the inner courtyard. Pretty impressive, but also probably quite a financial burden as to proper upkeep. Hence the elaborate event calendar. I stepped out of the truck and walked towards the main entrance.

To say I was nervous would have been the biggest understatement ever. I was sweating blood and water by now. Pulling open the front door and letting myself into the building meant passing a threshold from which there was no way back. Exposure and danger were lurking on the other side. But I did it. My hands shook only slightly, and my knees felt a bit like jelly, but my mind was all determined.

A lady barely older than I came down the stairs as I stood in the entrance hall, trying to remember where the armory was located.

"Are you a member of the gun class?" she asked friendly though without any greeting. She was pretty in an aloof way. As if she readied herself constantly to be photographed for fancy magazines. It made me feel frumpy.

"I hope to be so," I replied bravely and wondered whether she was the lady of the house.

She laughed a silvery little laugh that ended with a hiccup. "Let me guess. You have come on the spur of the moment without registering?"

I smiled sheepishly. "Exactly that, I'm afraid."

"Well, let me take you to our classroom, and I'll put in a word for you with my husband that you can join now and register during the break or at the end of the class." So, she *was* Mrs. Thornton! And so much younger than he, too. With a son barely twenty, she must have been just as old when he had snatched her up. And he must have been double her age back then. At least.

"Thank you!" My relief must have shown for she took the lead immediately and beckoned me to follow her.

We went through a maze of corridors that I vaguely remembered. Then, she stopped at an open door.

"Here we are. Just mingle, and I'll arrange for the rest," she smiled.

I stepped inside the room. A very plain and modern room with plenty of presentation technology and a round table in its center. Ten pairs of eyes tuned in on me. They all belonged to men of different ages, some of them very obviously city-bred and trying hard to look the country part. I would be the only woman in this class. So much for not standing out.

"Good morning," I said timidly. And timid I felt.

Meanwhile, I saw Mrs. Thornton catch her approaching husband by the elbow and quickly tell him about me. I saw him gaze in my direction, raise his brows, then nod, smile, and leave her on the threshold. She turned around. And then it was just him and us greenhorns.

"Good morning, everybody!"

We mumbled back a multi-staggered, "Good morning, Sir."

"Let's take seats at the round table and introduce ourselves. As you all know from your registration … or not …" Here he threw me a marked glance spiced with a twinkle in the corner of his eye, "My name is Richard Thornton. I'm the owner of this estate, and I also happen to be a hunter. I learned how to shoot as a kid already. Hunting and shooting are in my blood, so to say. So, please, introduce yourselves shortly and share why you are participating in this gun class for beginners. The lady first, maybe?"

My face grew hot. My mouth went dry. I swallowed hard and faked a bright smile. "Hi, my name is Emma Schwarz. Currently, I'm on vacation; but as a journalist I'm always keen on learning something new. So, I thought it can't get better than learning how to shoot and hunt on an English estate – so I might write an interesting piece about it in my hometown paper once I'm back to work again."

"You're aware, though, that you won't learn how to hunt in today's class, aren't you?" Mr. Thornton asked.

I just nodded, and the introduction round continued. There was an elderly, slightly pompous banker from London who had been invited by an investment partner to go hunting up in Scotland. A young man who wanted to be savvy when spending next summer on a ranch in Texas. An antiques dealer who simply wanted to be able to understand gun mechanisms and to be able to repair basic elements. A teacher, a butcher, a youngster barely out of his teens contemplating to become a policeman, a gun collector, an actor, a tattoo artist, and a guy into foraging and without any specific job description. In short – anybody you met in the street could be somebody interested in guns, shooting, and hunting. There went my cliché of aristocrats, gangsters, and rednecks.

"Good, now that we know a bit more of each others' background, what do you think comes first when you pick up a gun?"

"Loading it," suggested one guy.

"Checking whether it's loaded," interjected another.

Mr. Thornton swayed his head. "Any more ideas?" He looked around expectantly. Then he simply said, "Safety first."

"Ah," we all said cluelessly. But safety always sounded good.

"When you are handling a gun, make sure you are not pointing the barrel at any person or into any direction where a person could be. Which also means, before you pick up a gun, check the place for a safe direction to aim the barrel. In this room, for example, you best aim for the window. Why? Upstairs and downstairs as well as next door, there might be people. Outside this window, there is a long meadow without any path leading through or past."

We all nodded. Then followed instructions to make sure the magazine of the gun was not clipped in, whether the magazine was loaded, whether the safety was on, whether there was no cartridge stuck in the barrel, and – for heaven's sake – not to look down the barrel from the end through which the bullet passed out. To leave the finger off the trigger unless you were really meaning to shoot. Et cetera, et cetera. It wasn't exactly boring, but it was not really my first choice of topics either. Still, it might make for an interesting article for *VorOrt*, my newspaper in Filderlingen.

"I wonder when we will finally get to hold a real gun in our hands," one guy muttered under his breath. Another one just mumbled assent.

I kept my profile as low as possible although I couldn't wait to split from the group as soon as possible to find Michael. To ask him about Rose's background and whether his and her love story could be the reason for "killing the messenger", the person who was going to bring them together, Patrick Codona.

We learned about double and single action triggers, about muzzle loaders and the art of archery that started pervading game hunt. We learned about calibers and refilling cartridges. We learned about laws and about responsibilities. I took notes until I almost forgot what I had come here for; only I usually never took notes at all. I had a purpose of my own.

Then, finally, it was lunch time, and we were invited to a buffet in the adjacent room and to walk the premises. I went in with the group, making small talk, helping myself to some canapés and a few apple slices. Then I sauntered off behind four men who wanted to take a look at the kitchen garden, making it look like I belonged to the group. But I hung back before they went outside through a side door and, instead, slipped back and towards a staircase I had spotted on our way there. A quick glance around the hallway – nobody seemed to see me. And upstairs I went.

Of course, I had no idea of the layout of the manor and its wings except for what I vaguely remembered from the guided tour. We had only seen rooms that were open to the public for the tours. But I also had seen ropes hung with signs saying "Private". And that was where I was headed for.

My heart beat hard as I reached the second floor. Yes, there was a roped-off wing and also the roped-off continuation of the staircase to the third floor. I decided not to walk further upstairs but to risk entering the wing. I ducked under the rope and tiptoed towards the first door. I knew that tiptoeing wouldn't prevent me from getting discovered. I was in full sight in this slightly less well-kept hallway. Still, it made me seem safer. Slowly I turned the doorknob and pushed the door open. A private salon. I closed the door as quietly as I had opened it and crept on to the next …

An hour for luncheon and a walk was not long. One for an expedition such as mine seemed even shorter. I nervously checked my watch. I had to saunter back as leisurely as I had been walking off to cause no suspicion. How many more doors in this wing? I had already ended up in a boudoir and in a master bedroom. What next? Was Michael's room even on this floor? In this wing? Had I erred?

At the end of the wing, I turned to the other side of the hall and started opening doors there. And that's when I got lucky. I opened a door ... and immediately realized because of the decorative accessories that this was the young man's room. Sports trophies for "Michael Thornton". A photo of his graduation. Michael himself was not in the room, though. I turned my head, checked that nobody else was around, and sneaked in as fast as I could. I closed the door behind me and leaned against it for a moment to catch my breath.

Then, I looked around. This room presented a strange flair of 19th century elegance as to furniture, wallpaper, and textiles mixed with the comforts of this very century of ours, such as a radiator, halogen lights, a desktop, and a huge stereo center. I didn't know exactly what I was looking for. I'd have preferred it if Michael had been here and I could have talked to him. I was pretty sure that a chat between the two of us would even have been a good excuse to be late to the next part of the class whatever that was to be. As yet, I had to make do with the room minus its inhabitant.

There was no photo of Rose on the desk or on the nightstand. Clearly because Michael's father did not approve of the relationship, and any picture of her in the open would have been a provocation. How did the two lovers communicate with each other anyhow? By letter, I answered myself. Through Alan. That was what had been the case, at least, when I had last seen them at *The Bird in the Bush* on the same night. With a bit of luck, the letter Rose had handed Alan to deliver to Michael might still be around. But where?

I strode over to the nightstand – a heart's secret was often kept close to where one laid one's head and daydreamed. Journals, letters, poetry … No such luck. The nightstand held underwear, a broken-in box of condoms, and tickets for a show in Cambridge. I checked the date whether it could be some kind of meeting point between Michael and Rose. But no. The date was long in the past. Michael might just have kept the tickets as a keepsake. I paused.

"*The Purloined Letter*," I said to myself triumphantly. "Of course, that's what *I* would do in such a situation."

I flew over to Michael's desk. A quick look over the paperwork that was lying on top of it was disappointing. But then, there was the letter tray. I took the small pile of papers that lay inside and leafed through it. My fingers trembled. The sheets seemed to stick together to defy my effort. But then, finally, I came across a handwritten note in even but not yet fully developed, cursive handwriting. As soon as I read the first lines, I knew I had found what I was looking for. I took my flip phone and snapped a picture of the letter. Then I crammed everything back into the letter tray.

Five minutes later and just in time for class to resume, I walked down the hallway on the first floor again, softly humming. Nobody would be the wiser. I sat down at the table where I had left my notes.

"Did we lose you outside?" one of the group I had followed earlier asked me in a very low voice.

"No," I whispered back. "I forgot something inside."

He nodded understandingly, and the topic was done. I exhaled with relief. Nobody *was* the wiser.

19

After all of us had repeated the safety rules and been told that we should wash our hands and faces after shooting, as we would likely be covered in residue from the gunpowder and lead from the ammo, we all walked over to the armory.

"Before I hand each of you a rifle, are there any more questions?" Mr. Thornton asked.

"Can we book a hunt at your place right after this class?" the banker wanted to know.

"As in a direct follow-up?" Mr. Thornton's his smile seemed a bit condescending. "You'd have to check online whether there are still slots to be had. To my knowledge, we are fully booked through this season, already. – May I suggest to see how your shooting results will be today and then, maybe, take some practicing classes before you book a hunt?"

"Dang." The banker's face fell. "I had hoped to impress my host with some nice hunting stories.

"Why don't you invent one?" Mrs. Thornton had entered the armory behind us and smiled at the banker with flashing teeth and raised brows. Come to think of it, that had been the kind of smile she had given me when I had arrived this morning. It hadn't sat quite right with me, although she had sounded friendly and certainly had put in a word for me. "I started out like that until I was accepted into the men's club that shooting was back then.

After a while, I didn't have to make up stories anymore. I won every single trophy I wanted."

"I'm a man of numbers and facts, not tales," the banker mumbled.

"Are we going to shoot with birdshot or bullets?" I asked now.

"We are going to target-practice," Mr. Thornton answered.

"So, bullets," I stated and felt proud that I had nailed it. "What caliber are they?"

"They are .275s," Mr. Thornton replied. "We are shooting short range only, though. 100 yards. I want you to be able to check where you hit the target and improve your aim. We have an outdoor range back in the park. Its mound at the back hinders bullets from hitting anything beyond. Which is important, as such caliber can fly farther than a mile. You don't want to hit somebody out there, for sure."

We all laughed bashfully. As none of us had ever shot before, it might just be our luck to hit somebody or something we didn't mean to if it weren't for this mound.

"So, our bullets are in fact dangerous to people?" I ventured on, treading treacherous ground now. "Such as in being able to kill somebody?"

Mr. Thornton's face clouded over now. "There is no such thing as a harmless bullet, Ma'am. If you want harmless, this is the wrong class for you."

I blushed. The young actor next to me came to my rescue, though.

"I had the same question, Sir," he said with a playful whine. "I mean, we all have heard about people getting shot accidentally into the butt – with birdshot." If men can giggle, they did. "Now, a BB gun's ammunition easily shoots through thin metal, as I remember. A cousin of mine did it to my aunt's gutter back in the day – just for the fun of it and for the shooting pattern, mind. My aunt was not amused. Especially not after he did the same creative service to her car's passenger door. It looked decorative – at least to us kids. But it certainly sunk into the metal."

"Thank you for your contribution," Mr. Thornton said, and I wasn't sure whether his grin was really amused or rather sarcastic. "Indeed, pellets – which I presume your cousin shot – can do harm to all kind of surfaces and injure people, too. An eye is easily taken out by any object flying at a certain speed." He took a deep breath. Oh gosh, here comes, I thought. "Now, a .275 bullet will travel at about 3,000 feet per second – do the math yourselves. I don't think I have to tell you what this means when you hit anything living …"

"You'd kill yourself in a car hitting a wall at that speed," the aspiring Cowboy said lightly.

"Alright, any more questions?" All of us shook their head. "Well then, each of you gets a Rigby Highland Stalker – that's what these rifles in this rack are –, and mind to hold them in a way that is not dangerous to anybody visibly or invisibly around." Mr. Thornton grabbed the first one from the rack. "Emma, you get the ladies' version. It has a slightly shorter stock." Some of the guys snickered. "No need to be on the high horse, gentlemen. My wife shoots these with more accuracy than many a gentleman hunter could dream of."

He handed the gun to me, and I was surprised by the heaviness of the thing. Of course, the wooden stock was massive. I was wary what it would feel like going off. I had heard all kinds of things about recoils and bruises.

As the others were outfitted with their guns, I let my eyes wander across the room to check for anything out of the ordinary. The rifle displays on the long walls were fully intact, minus those that were handed out just now. But there was a gap in the cabinet with the vintage guns. Right between some revolvers and a large rifle. It felt like a punch to my gut. I stood too far away to walk up and check which gun was missing. Besides, walking over would have drawn attention to my purpose. Even taking out my flip phone to take a photo was an impossibility. I simply had to memorize the spot – which was easy enough, thank goodness! – and find a way to return later. Alone. Without witnesses.

Seemingly leisurely, I approached a table with gun literature, picked up one of the books, and – for convenience's sake – dropped my classroom notes in the empty spot. Then I buried my nose in the book for a few, and when everybody was finished, I simply placed the book on top of my notes. Grabbing my rifle at a safe angle, I followed the group outside.

It seemed like a mile's walk to the range to me. The men were walking purposefully, already some more confidence in their stride. Did carrying a gun make a man more male in his own eyes? Was it an old hunter instinct left over from when men were the providers for their tribes and families? To me the contraption of wood and metal with a trigger and hammer was a mere tool – to kill animals, to defend your nation against intruders. It didn't make me feel any better or worse as a person. It certainly made me wish I had stronger muscles.

There were a dozen benches at the range. We were shown how to use a bench rest and where to place our stools, as this was the easiest position for beginners to shoot. We were taught not to cross a specific line when the range was hot – which meant somebody was shooting at a target and one better not walk out into potential danger. We were shown how to load the magazines. We were handed ear plugs. We put on our safety glasses. And the show was on.

The first bump against my shoulder came as a bit of surprise. It wasn't as bad as I had feared. Like a friendly fist bump at most. My ears perceived the crack as more uncomfortable, though muffled by my earplugs. And I realized that my hands were shaking because I wanted to do well but didn't feel that this would ever become a favorite pastime of mine.

Of course, it was hit and miss, and I never counted how many rounds I loaded into my magazine and shot until the little box sitting on the bench next to me was empty. The guys right and left to me were doing pretty much as well or poorly as I but were far more excited by their activity, judging by how often the range went cold, so they could walk up to their targets and check where their bullets had hit.

Mr. Thornton walked up and down, correcting postures and giving tips. So, to my surprise, did Mrs. Thornton, who had joined us at the range.

"Because four instructor eyes see more than two," as her husband put it.

"You're not a bad shot," she encouraged me when my last bullet had been fired. "Want to join a ladies' class next week Saturday?"

I shook my head. "I'll not be around much longer."

"Oh?"

"I'm just a visitor."

"So, I *did* hear a slight accent!"

"German," I admitted. "I hope it's none too obvious."

"What made you take this class? I thought Germans were generally set against having guns and against shooting."

"Depends on whether they are hunters or not, I guess. As to me, I was looking for a story – I'm a journalist."

Did I see a shadow darken Mrs. Thornton's face for the fragment of a second? Or did I only imagine it? She quickly seemed to catch herself again and smiled brightly, "Well, I hope you have found yourself one that will be worth telling."

"Believe me, it will," I replied as cheerfully.

Boy, if I had only known …

20

When I turned Ozzie's truck into *The Heron's* driveway, there were three persons waiting for me outside the front door, two women and a man, all wearing hooded anoraks. I would have backed out and made a run hadn't one of them turned around. She looked at me, and I recognized Rose immediately. She urgently spoke to the two others, who turned around now, too. The man was none other than Michael. The other woman seemed vaguely familiar, but I wasn't able to place her.

I got out of the truck, locked it, and slowly walked over. I didn't know what to make of this encounter.

"Hi," I said warily. "You waiting for me?"

"Hi," Michael said. "Indeed, we are. We have been here twice already. Pretty much every hour. Can we talk?"

I unlocked the front door, still feeling uncomfortable. But curiosity won me over.

"Sure," I said. "Come in." I opened the door and let them pass inside. "How is your arm today?"

"Much better, thanks."

I led the three of them into the kitchen – it felt like more neutral ground, and I didn't want to let them intrude on Ozzie's privacy. I bade them sit at the kitchen table with a slight, inviting gesture. They took their seats and peeled themselves out of their anoraks.

"Coffee or tea anybody?"

"Tea would be fine, thank you," the unknown lady said.

As soon as I heard her voice, I made the connection and gaped.

"You are ..." Words failed me.

"The fortune teller from Newmarket, yes." She didn't smile. Her eyes looked very serious, instead. Sad even.

I shook my head in order to clear my thoughts. "But how come ...?" I waved across the little group, totally bewildered. Her strange prediction resounded in my mind. *Before you travel to another world for good, beware of bullets!* "How did you know where to find me? And what did you mean with what you said to me in Newmarket?"

She sighed softly. "I'm a fortune teller, aren't I?" I stared at her because I didn't believe she just said that as if it were the most obvious thought that would come to mind first. "I see you don't believe in clairvoyance." She clicked her tongue. "Well, too bad. But I'm serious. Although my name is *not* Miss Lola as the sign on my wagon says. It's a nom de plume, so to say. Just as the costume comes with the job. Just as the wagon comes with it. It's about customer expectation. In real life, my name is Esther Holland."

"Nice meeting you, Miss Holland."

"Oh, just call me Esther, please."

"Well, Esther ... I am ..."

"Emma Schwarz, a German journalist on vacation, house-sitting for a U.S. Air Force member." I felt my chin drop. "You found the towpath murder victim." I felt as if somebody had hit me over the head. "I did my homework before seeking you out. But don't get me wrong. I'm not usually visiting people whose fortune I have told. Although, sometimes I'm really curious how much of my predictions turns out to be true."

"So, you are not sure about what you are telling people?"

"I am," she insisted. "I cannot even tell you how I do it. Your friend – I think her name was Linda – was obvious as to where she came from and what she was about to do. She had a police badge and a photo of her sweetheart in her wallet. I saw them when she opened it to pay me. I was able to tell her these facts about herself very comfortably. But she lacked the aura to give her more than the common place predictions which are prone to come true anyway."

"Hah!" I exclaimed triumphantly. "I knew that they were common place predictions. I told her so. She just decided to hear what she wanted to hear."

Esther seemed to be a bit uncomfortable because she bit her lips and nodded slightly. "You are right, not everything in my business is about 'seeing' things. Mostly, I just tell customers the obvious in wording that they interpret. And surprise! It sounds like it is all their own truths. So, they walk away, happy. Your friend Linda was happy, wasn't she?" I nodded, kind of dazed. "There you go. It's some old trickery that comes with my trade. But there are those instances when something overcomes me and makes me say things. Predict things. And I don't know where they come from or where they might lead. They leave me exhausted, too. When that happens, I have to close up for the day."

"And that was the case with me?"

She nodded again. "I had no idea you had an American friend or that you would find a body, believe me."

"Well, if you had been able to predict the latter, you'd be suspect number one on my list now," I teased her. "So, you probably earn some pretty money with what you call trickery. Aren't you ashamed of pulling people's legs? Couldn't you do some more honest work?"

She didn't smile. "Fortune telling is but my storefront."

"I don't understand." I finally turned away from her, somewhat disappointed with her, filled the electric kettle with water, and switched it on.

"I'm working with the same Civil Rights group as Patrick Codona did," I heard Esther say to my back.

My head flew around. "You do what?!"

"Fortune telling is the cover I choose for finding people who might need help. And for taking them into my home until they are safe." She saw my disbelief. "It's not a trailer. I live in a decent home in a suburb of Cambridge – all year round. I used to be one of them. A girl who got married and was pregnant with a son at age seventeen. This group helped me get away, let me finish school, and set me up with a job. I decided to help as a volunteer. Patrick was the son of my best friend who was in a similar bad relationship. I managed to get both of them out; she went back after a while and never returned. Patrick stayed with me. He was like a second son."

Esther's eyes stayed dry. She gazed into a distant past.

"I knew that Patrick was supposed to get Rose and bring her to one of our group. He was supposed to pick up Rose after her shift was finished at *The Bird in the Bush* that night, drop her off, and then come back to my home. Alan had been the go-between and given Patrick the scarf as a sign of recognition. The night before, Patrick received a phone call from a woman who claimed to be Rose. Of course, now we know it wasn't Rose. She asked to be picked up during her break, in the afternoon. Patrick wasn't happy about this because he had to rearrange arrival times and security with a new safehouse. But he did. When he didn't return that night, I knew something had gone wrong."

Esther's eyes welled up, and Rose covered her hand, also tears in her eyes.

"I never changed the time of our meeting," Rose whispered. "I had no idea what had happened when I came to the towpath. I only saw that yellow tape, and I knew that something had gone dreadfully wrong. I also knew that I would have to get away from home because the arranged wedding was coming up quickly, and my father was so adamant."

Michael laid his healthy arm around Rose's shoulders protectively. What a sight this little group made. What fate connected them!

"You must think awful about my people," Esther finally said.

"I'm flustered," I admitted. "I don't really know what to think."

"We are like everybody else," Rose tried to explain. "We simply want to live our individual lives and be accepted as we are. With the same privileges everybody else enjoys. Unfortunately, we are still fighting for our rights on different levels. Because of our nomadic lifestyle a lot of institutions don't think that we fall into their realm of responsibilities. As we come and go, nobody thinks of us as part of the list of beneficiaries anywhere. That goes for the health system, and for education, and for so many more things. Even for the places we live. Some of us want to be part of the British society, just like I. I don't like being on the road all the time and hunkering down as invisibly as possible over winter because people don't care for our presence. I want to be a visible part with all the rights and responsibilities a sedentary citizen has. I study hard to pay my part to do so."

"But your father doesn't approve of it," I stated and placed mugs in front of everybody. The kitchen was silent for a moment until the kettle clicked to announce that the boiling process was finished. I rummaged through a cupboard and brought out the random choice of teas and tisanes that Ozzie had collected over the months. Then I placed the kettle and the tea sachets on the table and also sat down.

"My father wasn't always like this, apparently. At least, that's what some people told me when I encountered them during our times on the road. My mother was what my people call a Gorja." She looked at me as if to ask whether I understood what she was talking about. I nodded with a bitter, little smile. "She didn't like the way of life she had chosen in marrying him, after all. She ran away shortly after my birth and left me behind. It was easier for her, I guess. What triggered my father's change was that she took up with one of his family adversaries."

"Let me guess," I said tonelessly. "A Thornton?"

"Michael's father," Rose confirmed. "She became his lover. I don't know what she expected him to do. Marry her?!" Rose laughed scornfully. "I think Michael's father liked her beauty and secretly enjoyed cuckolding my father. Of course, my father heard the rumors about her all around the area. It must have hurt Michael's mother dreadfully, too. She had given her husband a son, and now she felt discarded. All because of whom they called a gipsy whore. I have been told that Mr. Thornton finally realized that the rumors didn't do *him* a favor either. It was not done to have a lover who was whispered about. So, apparently, one day he drove her to one of the bigger cities – Manchester or Birmingham, I heard both versions – and dropped her off. Chapter closed. And as a good and loyal wife, Mrs. Thornton stayed married. My father, though, had had it with people who deemed themselves so much better because they had a lighter skin and permanent homes. He returned to his ancestors' traditions. And that was it for me. I didn't know life could be different until Michael started befriending me at school. Before that, I had always thought I deserved being looked down on or considered 'exotic' as some allegedly more open-minded people called me. Michael was still a friend when we returned the next winter. And the next. He never wavered." Her big eyes looked at the young man with utter adoration and trust. "When I was taken out of school, he somehow managed to still see me. Although it became more and more difficult. When Michael heard that my father had promised my hand to a fellow Roma, he asked me to run away and marry him."

Esther broke the spell in simply placing sachets into everybody's mug and pour water over them.

"Do you have any sugar, perchance?" she asked as if we had just exchanged some platitudes.

I rose, got the sugar bowl from another cupboard, and brought it back to the table.

"So, you ran away."

Rose nodded. Silence fell over the room. I heard the grandfather clock from the living room, the humming of the fridge, a plane pass high over the roof. Michael dipped his sachet into the water and pulled it up again as if handling a fishing rod. Then he broke the silence.

"I grew up with my father's and mother's disdain against anybody traveling – be they Irish or Romany travelers. I never knew why. So, when Rose turned up in my class one day, I knew to keep my tongue in check about her. Unfortunately, this only worked for so long. I got my hide whipped more often than I can count for befriending whom they called a gipsy. And I spare you the adjectives that came with that. But I didn't care. I wanted to marry her sooner or later. Fate has it that sooner became necessary. Rose was working at Alan's place and he was good to her. So, I confided in Alan one day, as I had heard that he might be of help. Don't ask me how I got to hear it. When you move in certain gray areas, you will. Anyhow, Alan became the easiest connection between Rose and me when we needed to communicate. And he arranged for Rose's escape. Only, I never knew that he had to arrange it a second time after the first one had gone so tragically awry."

"That's when you came to the pub and asked where Rose was?" I interjected.

"Yes. And after all of the drama that enfolded then, Alan called me last night because he had found out where Rose had been brought. He had called one of Patrick Codona's phone numbers and ended up with Esther. She had only just found out about the towpath murder; she connected the dots for Alan. Who then told me. I drove over to Bury, where Rose's new safehouse was. We got married there on the spot, kudos to special permits, then went over to get Esther and to warn you of any further involvement in this case."

"I wasn't …," I began weakly.

But Ester silenced me with a dark look. "You *are* digging. Alan said so. And seeing you like this, I know that you have your own plans. Don't. Because I fear you might run into a deadly trap."

"The bullet about which you warned me?"

"I wouldn't know. But the voice that changed the time of the meeting didn't belong to Rose, as we all know now."

"Somebody spoke with a heavy accent that was suggesting a foreign background," Michael explained.

Rose just rolled her eyes. "Another cliché about us Roma," she said. Her English had been as English as it comes, the entire time. "People don't think we are able to talk English like everybody else. But it's what we grow up with, for heaven's sake!"

"So, who would have placed the call?" I asked tentatively. I felt my stomach roil, as I felt I already knew what they would tell me.

"The number …," Esther began.

But Michael shook his head. "This one is on me." Then he turned to look at me. "The call came from the office phone at Balmer Hall, of all places. It can only have been my mother."

21

"Hi, girlfriend," Linda said cheerfully. "How are things in the land of bangers and mash?"

I had barely dressed the following morning and made some coffee when the home phone rang. I knew it wouldn't be Ozzie and that, therefore, it could only be Linda. Or Barb, come to think of it. But we had separated before the interrogations at the police station, and since then, there had been no need nor time for Barb to talk to me about anything. That is, from my point of view. I had stated everything I had witnessed. She would have compared her findings with Alan and my report – and that would have been it. Nothing enlightening, unless Alan had spilled some beans I didn't know about.

So, I grabbed the receiver and my mug, shuffled to the living room, and dropped into Ozzie's timeworn armchair.

"Hi, Linda! Things are great!"

"In spite of Ozzie's deployment?"

I teared up a bit but swallowed the pain as quickly as possible. "Well, it *is* hard. It feels like I can never get enough of him. Every time we have just gotten used to each other's company, we get interrupted again."

"Long distance relationships," Linda said, her voice dripping with pity. "On the other hand, it never gets old for you, does it? Do you even ever build up to a fight?"

"Nope," I laughed. "No time for that, either. Not that I'm keen on fighting with Ozzie."

"See, Steffen and I bicker all the time. And yesterday, we had our first real big fight."

"Oh my! About what?"

"Honeymoon destinations, wedding costs, guest numbers. I almost called it off."

"What?! The wedding? No!!!"

"Well, I gave in, in the end. I didn't want to lose this handsome, sexy guy. And he is so different from all the other partners I've ever had."

"And don't I know that?!" Indeed, Linda had always fallen fast and hard for anybody who seemed remotely interested in her. After they had gotten from her what they'd wanted, mostly a one-night stand, they'd usually let her down as fast and hard, and Linda had been constantly been upset about herself, deeming herself not worthy of true love. Until she had met Steffen. He could have gone down the same road with her as everybody else had. I hadn't given him the benefit of the doubt, at first. But he had turned out to be the real deal. So, a row about the wedding was something really serious.

"What was the compromise?" I asked. "Because I assume a compromise it is?"

Linda sighed. "We are going to make it a smallish affair. I'm still trying to get over it. Instead of 300 guests, there will be only a hundred."

I gasped. "300?! I didn't even know you had that many friends!"

"Well, count Steffen's riding people, my office, most of my Facebook friends, …"

"Your what?! Facebook friends? Are you serious?!"

"Well, I was. Until Steffen asked me whether I had even met all of them. I have to admit that he got me there. So, I had to cut down that list quite a bit. And I had to obliterate the police station. And the riding people."

"Okay, that sounds reasonable."

"It hurts, though," Linda pouted. "And what will they think about not being invited?"

"Most of them will probably not have expected to be invited," I consoled her.

"Hmph."

"No, really! And do you think that all the so-called influencers you befriend would have come?"

"Well, with the agenda we had, I'm sure they would have," Linda wailed.

"Oh, so the agenda has been cut down, too?"

"Steffen agreed on the wedding ceremony in a chapel," she sighed. "Not on horseback. And there will be only a few horse people in hunting uniforms. There will be no application for fireworks at night, and the champagne reception has turned into one with simple bubbly."

"Well," I laughed, "to be honest I like bubbly way more. And as to the rest of it all – Linda, that wouldn't have been you, anyhow!"

"No?" she whimpered.

"No. You are gorgeous yourself, and all that whoop dee would have placed you in the background. It would have been more about all the show than about you and Steffen."

"That's what he said, too," she admitted.

"There you go. Besides, you might be able to say at least hello to every single person of your hundred guests. You would still be shaking hands by dinner time with 300 of them." I heard her giggle. "It's not about size but about quality, you know."

"Yeah, maybe you are right."

"I know I am. You'll be glad you have it smaller and cozier once you get there."

"Let's hope so. – Change of topic. What are *you* up to these days? Anything new going on in the village of Ealingham? And has Scotland Yard found the murderer?"

"You mean the Criminal Investigation Department."

"Yeah, well. Have they?"

I wasn't sure how much I wanted to tell Linda. On the other hand, it was never bad to have a pro tell you whether your train of thought was correct or not. Where to change it if necessary. Though, of course, never have them tell you to sit back, relax, and let somebody else do the job.

"I took a gun class at Balmer Hall yesterday," I began on the most harmless path I could choose.

"You?! A gun class?!" Linda giggled. "That's so *not* you."

"Hold your horses," I warned her. "I'm the girlfriend of somebody in the U.S. Air Force, after all."

"You told me once that Ozzie said the moment he as a maintenance guy would have to wield a gun was when the situation was really beyond reparable. So, don't give me that bull!"

I sighed. "True. I just wanted to become more knowledgeable about guns."

"Right," Linda scoffed. "And the only way to do so is taking a gun class. Not going to a library and reading up on it, or googling stuff on the internet."

"Do I hear sarcasm?"

"Well, you tell me!" I stayed silent. "Are you trying to tell me that your sudden interest in gun classes has nothing to do with the towpath murder? At Balmer Hall, of all places?"

"What's wrong with Balmer Hall?"

"Isn't that the place Ozzie took you the other day? And you told me in no uncertain terms that you were bored to death in the armory whereas Ozzie was all enthusiastic about the vintage guns they showed in one of the glass cases?"

"Yeah, well …"

"Why Balmer Hall? Why at all?"

"Because it's close by."

"And ...?"

"There is a connection to the body I found," I admitted lamely.

"I knew it!" Linda exclaimed. "I just knew that you couldn't leave well enough alone."

"Not my fault the facts are piling up on me."

"Well, if you stopped digging where it is none of your business, they'd stop doing so!"

"I was not really digging when I was at the pub with Ozzie and witnessed Rose and Michael Thornton."

"Who is Rose?"

"The girl the guy was going to help before he was killed."

"Hm."

"And Michael is her lover. No," I corrected, "he is her husband now. And he belongs to Balmer Hall."

"Then why isn't he called Balmer?"

"You ask *me* that."

"And where is the logic of it all?"

I realized that I had to go into more detail for Linda. It was a bewildering story, and I would have to do my best and relate it to her chronologically. So, I started; but in a way, it was still like a piece of Swiss cheese. There were still quite a few holes in the narrative. I didn't have any real proof. Except ...

"I found this letter in Michael's room." Silence. "Linda, you still there?"

"Very much so," she replied icily.

"What's the matter?"

"Didn't I tell you to keep away from the body?"

"I wasn't anywhere near. Scouts' honor."

"You have never been a scout."

"Touchée. But seriously, I'm not keen on the company of dead bodies really."

"Very funny," Linda replied. "So, you use a lunch break to break and enter."

"There was no breaking. The door was unlocked."

"Great. But you went around the rope."

"Under it, to be precise. And yes, I entered the room to chat with Michael and find out how he was doing the day after he had been injured by that flying splinter." Linda didn't say anything. "Okay, and maybe to find out a bit more about the background of the entire story."

"You should have left immediately once you saw that he was not even there."

"Well, but I was there, and why not make the best of this situation?!"

"You call this the best?"

"Will you just listen? Please? Because I found something way better than any presumptions that Michael might or might not have had at that time."

"What did you find?"

"A letter from Rose. In his letter tray."

"A letter …"

"My guess is that it was the same letter Rose handed to Alan that night I was at the pub with Ozzie and that Michael picked up only shortly afterwards. Do you want me to read what's in there?"

"Spare me a love letter ..."

"It's not." I grabbed the print-out that I had left on the coffee table in the living room. "It says, *Dearest, I'll make my escape with Alan's guy's help after my shift on Thursday night. Call one of his numbers below around 10 p.m. He will tell you where to find me. Love, Rose.'* – Now, if I was able to find this letter so easily, guess who else might have."

"Basically, anybody who had access to his room. A cleaning woman, for example."

"Is that all you come up with after all I have told you?!" I couldn't believe that Linda didn't see what I had seen in the letter and its location.

"Okay, okay. But this is just you assuming that one of his parents found the letter."

"Actually, it's not just that," I countered. "There was a witness to the call that changed the time of Rose's meeting. And this witness not only realized recently that this call by a woman was fake. It also came from the office of Balmer Hall."

"What office?"

"The one where they do all the office work ... Really, Linda! Isn't it obvious that it was Michael's mother who called?"

"Or formerly mentioned cleaning woman ..."

"Why would she … Oh, Linda, please! The guy, I mean, Patrick Codona was shot the afternoon after the call. And probably not by the cleaning woman."

Linda sighed. "So, you have your story together now. But you still have no proof."

"There was a gun missing from the vintage exhibit when we were in the armory and received our rifles for the gun class, yesterday."

"There might be a simple explanation," Linda tried.

"My guess is that it is the gun Codona was shot with. I wasn't able to check which one."

"That's too bad." I wasn't sure whether Linda was mocking me or whether she was seriously concerned.

"And that's why I'm driving over to Balmer Hall this morning."

"Are you kidding me?! You are not going to go there again! This is plain stupid."

"It would be stupid not to," I contradicted. "You can't let a murderer stalk around and possibly do more harm. Besides, I need to prove that Mr. Buckland was not the murderer."

"Great. Simply great. And, of course, you already have a plan how to accomplish this."

"I do," I said.

"Is there any class or guided tour today, at all? Mondays museums are usually closed." I heard the triumph in Linda's voice. She clearly didn't think it possible that I enter Balmer Hall without official registration and get my way.

"No," I answered truthfully. "But I made sure that I will be able to get straight back into the armory and check the label of the missing gun."

"How?"

"I left a notepad there. My notes for the article I told them about."

"You never take *any* notes on anything!"

"But they don't know this. Do they, now?"

22

After I had hung up and finished my breakfast – I made it a large one, as I didn't know how long my errand might take me –, I wrapped myself in my coat, scarf, knitted hat, and gloves and set out into the frosty November morning. The sun had barely made it through the morning clouds, and its light was a pastel-yellowish shimmer rather than a full winter blaze. Nature glittered like a thousand diamonds. I had to clear the truck windshield off a rather thick layer of heavy crystals. With fingertips numb in spite of the gloves, I finally climbed inside and started the motor.

Ealingham was all quiet. It was as if the houses were still asleep, although it was a Monday morning. The only birds I could spot were crows, and they seemed to be content sitting on rooftops or telephone poles. There wasn't even a single other vehicle. The world held its breath …

Instead of thinking of what lay ahead and maybe in wait for me, I concentrated on the roads. When I reached the great gate of Balmer Hall – thank goodness, it was open –, I exhaled. Now just to get into the armory.

Had they observed me from the windows? Or had my truck made enough noise to call attention to my arrival? As soon as I reached the front door, it was opened as if by magic. It was an elderly man in an impeccable butler outfit. He hadn't been there yesterday for the arrival of our gun class.

"Good morning," I said more cheerfully than I felt.

"Good morning, Ma'am," he replied without a single emotion to his face. Were butlers trained the immobility of their features? And this seemingly elitist sneer? He carried it out to perfection. "How may I help you?"

"I am a member of yesterday's gun class. Unfortunately, I forgot the notes I took for an article I plan to write. I wonder whether I might have a look where I could have left them. Possibly in the armory."

The butler stepped back and held the door open for me to enter.

"Please, wait here," he said. "I'll inquire with the Thornton family whether anything was found."

This was not going according to my plan. I had assumed that I would be able to make my way to the armory without being intercepted by anybody. Foolish, of course, as outside tours and classes, this still was a private property.

"I know the way to the armory," I ventured.

"Just a moment, please," he insisted and strode towards the hallway in which yesterday's classroom had been located. As he didn't look back and I simply wanted to make headway, I sprinted off to the armory. I was lucky to find it unlocked. But then, of course, they had a Cerberus at the door who would have prevented any uninvited intruders from trespassing. Except me. I headed straight for the glass cabinet in which the vintage arms were exhibited, cellphone switched to photo mode.

And I held my breath. The empty spot in the cabinet was … filled again. Which one had been the gun missing?

I scanned the wall from one side to the other. So, the muzzleloader Ozzie had pointed out to me had still been there yesterday. I was pretty sure about it. I hadn't really expected it to be the missing gun, anyhow. It shot no cartridges but plain bullets, and loading time between shots took way too long for any quick shooting action. No premeditated murder would involve such a gun. But the gap had been to its left. I remembered because of the revolvers on its other side. I checked the sign under the gun. It read *US M1917 "Enfield"*. This was not the gun I had thought to be missing. What caliber did this one shoot? I took a photo of the cabinet and one close-up of the gun and the sign. I would have to look into this gun more closely as soon as I got back to Ealingham again.

"And what do you think you are doing in here, unaccompanied?" Mr. Thornton asked behind me. I whirled around.

"I was waiting for you until I could browse through the books over there. So, you'd see I'd not take anything away. Except the notes I left here accidentally, yesterday."

"And meanwhile you were doing what exactly? Why didn't you simply wait in the hall as requested?"

"I didn't want to steal anybody's time and hoped your employee might come back with the permit to go through the books. Meanwhile, I was taking photos of your vintage arms. My partner just seemed to love their looks the other day," I smiled brightly.

"Why have you been focused on this specific gun, though?"

"A ..." I turned around and read the description. "A US M1917 'Enfield'. Does that mean it is from World War I?" I turned around again.

"It does." Mr. Thornton had come closer.

"What caliber does it shoot, anyway?" Might ask now, just as well.

"30-06. It was an American gun distributed to the British home guards. We had to use the US caliber, as there was no time to modify the gun for our British ammunition."

"Interesting. Yesterday it was missing, though. Why?" I blabbed, as it sagged that this gun used the exact same ammo as an M-1 and might well have been the murder weapon. "Was something wrong with it? Did you have to repair anything?"

"Ah, but you know that all too well, already, don't you?" Mrs. Thornton had entered the armory through the other door, and I was now standing between husband and wife. Her eyes were glittering with hatred. "I knew something was feeling wrong, yesterday. No tourist from Germany comes over here to take a gun class. You are after something else."

I tried to play it cool, but I wasn't sure whether I succeeded. "I was trying to learn something new. That is not forbidden, is it?"

"Depends on what you wanted to learn. Apparently, it has nothing to do with shooting but all with a missing gun in our cabinet. But it was never missing."

"Was it used lately, perchance?"

Her laugh was shrill and betrayed that she didn't feel too sure of herself, either. Then she came a bit closer. "Why would I tell you?"

"Because you might just as well," I dared her. "I found you out. *You* found Rose's letter in your son's room and called the number it gave, pretending you were Rose. Your fake accent should have given you away, but your later murder victim didn't know Rose personally and assumed that this is how she actually spoke. Then you asked to meet him in the afternoon in order to hinder Rose's escape. You called out to him, then shot him. But you overlooked that the scarf in his hands would give away his connection to Rose."

"Well done!" Mrs. Thornton clapped her hands and walked around me, closing in. "You figured it all out."

"The only thing I haven't figured out is your motif. What made you shoot a perfect stranger? Why this brutal opposition against Rose's marriage to Michael?"

Mr. Thornton just stood there, pale and very calm. God only knew what he might be thinking. I got the impression that he hadn't been in the picture about what had happened. To think that he had been another suspect of mine! Mrs. Thornton, by now, was wild-eyed. She slipped her hand into the pocket of her jacket and pulled out a small revolver.

"Don't, Eve," Mr. Thornton said quietly.

But she didn't seem to hear or didn't want to hear. I stared at her small gun, the slender hand with its long fingers holding it ever so casually. Too casually. As if it didn't mean anything to her whether she pointed the barrel at anybody or not. Of course, she had already killed somebody. What more damage could a second murder do? A lifetime sentence would only double in theory. She only *had* this one life – she might as well go for more kills. I shuddered.

"You, my sweetheart," she hissed at her husband, "you and her slutty mother are the reason I killed that man. No son of mine is marrying the daughter of the woman who ruined my marriage. I won't have a constant reminder of this awful time under my roof or anywhere at family reunions. With offspring that also would remind me of how treacherous man can be!"

"So, you killed the messenger," I stated and wasn't sure whether I pitied the woman more than I disdained her. Her murder might have been cold-blooded; her motif certainly was not.

"He wasn't able to bring her to my son anymore."

"But somebody else stepped in," I pointed out. "They are now married."

She wailed. "My son, my beautiful, foolish son!"

Suddenly, she aimed the revolver at her husband. He stepped back, lifting his hands.

"Don't, Eve!"

In walking backwards, Mr. Thornton stumbled over a humidifier by the other door and crashed into the wall. He had barely managed to break his fall when a shot rang out. His eyes grew large, his hand flew to his shoulder, where petals of red started to soak his shirt.

"It's all your fault!" Mrs. Thornton screamed. "My mother warned me before our wedding. Said that somebody this old marrying somebody my age would go for those even younger, all the time, as I would grow older. She was right. Good Lord, I was only twenty back then, but that girl was apparently even more attractive. How I hated the whispers and the looks of pity wherever I went. And now I should have the daughter of hers under my very eyes, each and every day until the day I die?!"

She turned around to me, again. I had moved towards the other doorway very quietly, in order to make an escape. But now, she pointed the barrel at me, and all I could think was that I couldn't just die. Not here, not now. This was not the way my story should end. There was still so much to do. I was to have a life with Ozzie. Oh Ozzie, this would never have happened if you had been around!

"And you, Miss Smarty-Pants, you had to dig around where you had no business to be. I'm afraid this is it for you."

Should I bluff and attack her despite the gun she aimed at me? How many bullets did this thing hold? Would I die if she hit me with a round or two? Or should I just turn around as fast as possible and run? What were the chances of getting hit in the back? Because she *would* shoot, no matter whether I was facing her or not, wouldn't she?

I stared at this demon woman with her hair so slick and well-coiffed, her skin now mottled with hectic blotches of red. The longer I concentrated on her, the more blurred everything around her became. I tasted iron in my mouth. The flavor of mortal fear.

"Drop your gun! Now!"

The shout came at the same time as the crack of a shot. I was violently pushed to the ground and hit my head at the corner of the cabinet that held the vintage guns. For a moment, I lost my vision and only sensed the tumultuous scene that enfolded around me.

When I finally opened my eyes, I heard somebody call, "Officer down!"

A pastel-pink pant suit wooshed past me and then knelt down next to me. Detective Superintendent Barb Tope. She was seeing to Sergeant Cameron, who was lying on the wooden floor, blood running from a wound in his shoulder and cussing through grinding teeth.

"Let me see," she said as calmly as possible and gently began to probe his shoulder.

Sergeant Cameron winced. Barb gazed at me sideways and didn't say a word. But her eyes told me fairly well what she thought of my presence at the armory of Balmer Hall. I bit my lips.

My head throbbed, and my hand went for what I knew would grow into a hefty bump. Again. It wasn't bleeding. But it hurt like hell.

Meanwhile, a policeman read the handcuffed Mrs. Thornton her rights and led her out of the room. I heard sirens approach the estate. They were stifled as soon as I heard the gravel crunch under car wheels. There were short, urgent calls and quick steps nearing the armory. And then, the room was swarming with medics.

I saw Mr. Thornton being placed on a gurney. Sergeant Cameron had sat up with Barb's help; another medic wound a tourniquet around his arm and then accompanied him outside.

"No worries, you will look fine again in a couple of weeks," Constable Williams cheered me up. He almost seemed to enjoy the situation. "Place an old steak on it as soon as you can."

"Thanks," I said and bit my lips.

"Sergeant Cameron saved your life, you know," Barb said as she walked past me.

I rose from my position on the ground and ran after her.

"Barb! I can explain everything!"

She stopped in her path and looked at me over her shoulder.

"No more words from you, please! I won't even put your name in any report. If I did, you'd have to hang around for even longer and probably cause even more havoc. Be glad I let you off the hook."

She rushed outside, her lilac scarf flying. I was left behind with the forensic guys who secured another crime scene.

"May I ask you to leave, please?" The butler looked down his nose at me. I had no idea when he had emerged from the hallway.

I nodded shortly, accepting that he took over for his employer for the time being, and slowly walked outside the magnificent mansion that had held so much misery.

23

"Why did I know you'd come back with a bump to your head, Miss Marple?"

Niko Katzakis, my crime reporting colleague with *VorOrt*, the daily paper in Filderlingen that I was writing for, inspected me with twinkling eyes. He seemed to have a hard time not to laugh out loud. His suppressed mirth lent his tan face some extra color, and his dark curls moved like Medusa's snakes as we were walking back from "the loft", as we called our editor-in-chief Hannes Ginster's spacious office-cum-conference room, to our respective offices.

"Not funny," I muttered.

"I couldn't imagine being thanked in a more charming way," he teased.

"Thanks for nothing," I grumbled. But I couldn't help it – my mouth split into a grin. "I mean it."

"Well, it's not every day that Scotland Yard calls you about a colleague to figure whether they are the real deal. And then you get yourself involved in a shoot-out. Sort of. Crazy!"

"Well, I had no clue Barb would call you. And you had no business calling Linda afterwards. That wasn't fair at all."

"Well, but in the end, it came in handy that Linda knew what you were up to. And that she kept calling you over there to check how things were going. Because if she hadn't called me and told me that you were sneaking back to Balmer Hall, I couldn't have called Barb and let *her* know. And this means she wouldn't have moved heaven and earth to get a SWAT team to your rescue. And Hannes would have to word an obituary about the woman who set her foot where angels fear to tread."

"Bahaha," I grimaced. "SWAT team. That's a good one. It was the village police along with a few from Mildenhall or so. And yes, I know it was very thoughtful of Linda to warn you of what she called my shenanigans. And even more thoughtful of you to make a call to Barb and let her know that I had crossed her red line. You should have seen the look she gave me when the arrest was finally over and done with."

"You have to admit you deserved every bit of it." Niko invited me into his office with a wave. I entered and sat down on the edge of his desk, there being no second chair.

"Guilty, your honor," I admitted. "But it hurt when she left me off the hook just like this, and not the least bit of my involvement being acknowledged."

"You said it yourself that if she hadn't done this, you'd still be sitting over there, maybe even in a witness box at court. And they might let you have it worse for interfering with a police investigation."

"I was *not* interfering. I was helping," I pointed out.

"Have it as you will. – But say, Barb said she'd have gone in with or without my call, anyhow. Any idea on that? I mean, since I know your side of the story, I'd love to know what *she* had on Mrs. Thornton."

I shrugged. "You know, it's all piecemeal to me. Barb didn't hook up with me anymore. When I returned to the pub that night, she had already paid for her room and was gone. So, everything I got was from Sergeant Cameron, whom I visited at the hospital in Ely the day after, of course."

"Was he badly wounded?"

"Thank goodness, he's expected to make a full recovery," I sighed. "But he lost a lot of blood. It was he who pushed me to the ground. He took the bullet for me. He's a real hero. That was the best part of my visit to him, anyway – he was totally happy to go out with a bang, as he called it. Even though the murder case per se was out of his hands and he was considered just a 'support', he made it into the headlines as a super-hero."

"Great," Niko muttered. "Headlines are fine. But I'm not sure I'd want them at all cost."

"Well, each to their own."

"So, was it he who gave you Barb's side of the story?"

"Yes. He said she was spot-on in her investigations. Tough as nails, too. In spite of her really bad cold, she must have worked like a horse. She had insisted that they find somebody to get into Codona's smartphone which he carried on him. When she heard the accent of the message about changing the meeting times, she apparently suspected immediately that it was fake. She also had her people work on guns that shoot 30-06 center fire cartridges. It didn't take *her* long to figure that there are two types of vintage guns that do and to check the area for gun owners of either kind. The bullet turned out to have DNA of Codona on it – ugh, I don't even want to think of the matter that might have still clung to it!" I made a gagging sound.

Niko laughed. "It might have been miniscule to invisible. – So, did she really *know* that Mrs. Thornton was the killer?"

"You know, that was really the strangest thing. She went in but didn't have any more proof than I did. Less in fact, as Esther Holland, Rose, and Michael had never paid her a visit. Alan was wary of Barb after his interview and didn't want them to have to deal with similar." Niko wanted to say something, but I lifted my hand to stop him. "Of course, Barb had more than enough reason to arrest Mrs. Thornton once she arrived at Balmer Hall. I mean, that woman had just shot her husband and tried to shoot me as well. Only, it was Sergeant Cameron who caught it. The rest must have been super-easy. Mrs. Thorntons little revolver and the case I found both bore Mrs. Thornton's fingerprints."

"The case as well?"

"Of course." Niko looked bewildered. "It had to be loaded into the magazine, duh!"

"Ouch. Of course."

"Plus, the bullet turned out to bear the marks of the US M1917 'Enfield' from the gun cabinet in the armory."

"Neat. What about Mr. Thornton? Did she kill him?"

"No. But the bullet got stuck in a bone, and it must be a long and painful journey for him to recover."

"Do you think she injured him this way on purpose?"

I pondered it for a second. "Well, I think it is possible. He caused her a lot of pain back in the day. And according to Mr. Buckland he was as vicious a brute to his family as any of the Thorntons before him. All jovial to outsiders, though. Also, Mrs. Thornton let me know that she has quite a collection of shooting trophies. Yes, she might have planned a shot that would cause more pain than danger to him. In her way, she probably still loves him, after all."

"All is fair in love and war," Niko quoted.

"I don't think this applies to anything involving guns."

Niko winked. "She might have thought so, though. What about Mr. Buckland?"

"Yeah, what of him … He must be shocked that the wedding he arranged will never take place and that Rose got her way, after all. Because of his traveling life-style, they didn't set bail for him, and he is still in custody, awaiting trial. Michael told me he is not going to go after him, as that wouldn't be a good basis for family bonds. Father-in-law and all that. As to Alan – he said he'd be fine if the damage to the bar was paid. He doesn't want to make it difficult for Rose either – in the end, she used to be one of his most reliable employees. And he wanted to help her, not harm her family."

"So, all's well that ends well," Niko stated.

"Yeah, sort of."

"Huh?"

"Linda gave me an earful the day after all of this happened at Balmer Hall. She had tried to reach me all Monday afternoon. Then she went to the internet and found that there had been a shooting at Balmer Hall with several people injured. And I wasn't back at *The Heron* – that's the name of Ozzie's home – until shortly before midnight. She was in a frenzy and thought I lay in a coffin somewhere in forensic pathology."

"They don't use coffins there. It would have been a metal tray, a thin blanket, and a string around your toe with a paper note stating your name," Niko chuckled.

"Thank you for enlightening me."

"And what about Ozzie? Does he know already what you got yourself into?"

I hopped off the desk and walked towards the door. On the threshold I turned around.

"You know, I have the feeling that you really enjoy that everybody berates me. Yes, he is back. Yes, he knows. No, he is not favorably impressed, and he told me that if I wanted to get myself killed, I could have had it easier than waiting for the next criminal case I could jump on. – Why doesn't anybody ask me how *I* am feeling?"

"Aaw, Miss Marple," Niko faked pity. "I keep the best for last. But I imagine you are pretty distraught that you won't win any beauty contest in the next couple of weeks or however long it takes for that bump of yours to shrink and lose its manifold colors.

And I presume that it is still pretty painful though not immediately dangerous to your life."

"Thank you for your commiseration."

"Anytime, anytime."

I showed him my tongue and left. A moment later, I sat down in my shoebox-sized office in the attic and rifled through my mail tray. There was a letter with a British stamp. I turned it over, but it showed no return address. I slit the envelope with the handle of the spoon with which I used to stir my coffee, and turned it upside down.

A photo fell out. It showed a very pretty young bride and groom in wedding regalia. The note attached to it read, *"Thought you might like a reminder of what this was all about. Safe travels, always. Esther"*.

Epilogue

"I herewith declare you husband and wife. – You may kiss the bride."

I was sobbing, and my face was probably a mess. Ozzie tenderly held my hand while rummaging in his jacket for a handkerchief. When he found it, I decided not to take it – it was white, and my mascara, by now running into the corners of my mouth, would have soiled it irreversibly.

It was March, and all the things Linda and Steffen could have wished for their wedding day had come true. The weather was mellow for this time of year. The sun was out, the birds were singing, the lawn around Solitude Palace was a lush green, and the trees in the entire area began unfolding their budding leaves. The few children among the guests were well-behaved. The horses that had drawn the carriage to the foot of the curved staircase had refrained from popping road apples on the cobble stones. Linda's wedding dress had come out of the carriage uncrumpled, and Steffen had waited at the altar with a dreamy look for which I almost envied Linda. Ozzie was way more matter of fact when it came to gazing at me. But he had to go through a lot more with me than Steffen did with Linda.

Ozzie had visited me shortly after his return from his Moroccan deployment. I had braced myself for a curtain lecture. But none had come. He had just looked at my still very colorful temple and sighed.

"You're not going to reprimand me?" I asked, surprised.

"You are a grown-up person. I can't keep you from doing what you're doing, obviously. And anything I'd say wouldn't undo your involvement in that murder case either. So ..."

That had taken me down by a notch or two, much more than any sterner reproach he could have thought of.

"I promise I won't ever ..."

But Ozzie had just lifted his hands. "Don't. You may think now that you'd keep your promise – but you will break it later. You simply missed your vocation. You ought to have become a detective."

I had bitten my lips. Then I had admitted, "But writing reports is not half as fun as writing a real good story that gets read by so many more people."

He had shaken his head in mock despair, then pulled me towards him and kissed my bump. This had felt ever so good – soothing, soft, cool.

We hadn't been able to spend Christmas together. For me, January had been a month of visiting consumer and trade fairs in the area and reporting about them. In February, Ozzie had been deployed to Kirgizstan, of all places. I had read up and learned as much as I could about that nation as I always did when he was traveling. I had changed our telephone schedule to accommodate his strict military agenda in yet another time zone.

In between, Linda had dropped her and Steffen's invitations on us. Thick white paper with an embossed golden

Cinderella carriage inside a laurel wreath. It was a bit over the top, and I didn't even know what a laurel wreath had to do with a wedding. But I assumed that this was a compromise of Steffen's, who had curbed so many of Linda's highfalutin plans for their special day. Ozzie had immediately taken some days off to make it to Stuttgart Airport a couple of days early.

It had been raining cats and dogs the morning he arrived with the first German Wings flight from Stansted. We had rushed through the torrent to the parking garage, still getting thoroughly wet. My yolk-colored beetle had done its best to dry us out during the ride home to my apartment in Filderlingen, but our clothes had still been uncomfortably humid when I had finally unlocked the door.

A change of clothes and a Swabian brunch with pretzels, rolls, and all kinds of cold cuts and cheeses later, we had finally felt cozy enough to talk plans for the following days. And that was, when Ozzie had dropped a bombshell.

"I'm going to go back to the States next year, again."

"What?"

"You heard me alright. I have tried to prolong my stay in Mildenhall by another year. But no such luck. They will send me back anyhow. My four-year tour will be up."

I had felt as if the ground had dropped from underneath my feet. My voice had sounded strangled to myself when I had asked, "Do you know where?"

"No idea yet," Ozzie had said, and he had looked glum. "They will give me a list of eight or so bases to choose from. But that doesn't mean that I get a say. They will place me where they need me."

"This is so unfair," I had whispered, and now my floodgates had opened. "We have only just started our relationship."

"I know. But it can't be helped."

By now, I had been weeping without restraint, and he had held me in his arms, helpless himself.

This was the mood in which we had arrived at Solitude Palace. A mix of happiness for our friends to get married and utter despair about the plans some government institution had devised for Ozzie's and my future. I had smiled bravely when Linda had walked down the aisle of the baroque chapel. She probably hadn't even really seen me – her eyes had been fixed on Steffen, and her veil must have misted everything in something like white vapor. Her dress was even more overdone than the one she had criticized back in Newmarket. All sequins, beads, rhinestones, and lace. Not to talk of a train at least three yards long. When she had folded back her veil at the altar, everybody had been able to see her radiant smile. It had been contagious. At least for the duration of the service and the ceremony itself, I had been able to push my heartache to the back of my mind. Until the end of the actual ceremony.

Here I sat, bawling like a baby. And Ozzie, my knight in shining armor, insisted on wiping my tears, mascara included, with his formerly white, now grayish handkerchief.

"To think this isn't even *our* wedding," Ozzie whispered into my ear teasingly.

My chin dropped. "Did you just propose to me?"

"I wouldn't dream of ruining this wedding by a public announcement." He looked me in the eye. "But indeed, this wedding is inspiring. And a wedding involving the two of us might solve our little problem. What do you say?"

I looked into Ozzie's hyacinth-blue eyes. They were filled with warmth and ... Did he really look at me, all dreamy?!

"Yes," I whispered. "Oh, yes."

We waited with our sealing kiss until the church was nearly empty.

"Uhm," somebody behind us harrumphed. It was the pastor who had held the service. "Is there another booking in the cards?" Ozzie actually blushed, and I giggled nervously. "You know where to find this chapel's number?"

We just nodded and fled outside, holding hands.

"We seem to look the part," Ozzie finally said as we found our place in the big group photo that Linda had insisted on.

"Clairvoyants and prophets seem to have taken our side," I smiled. "Looks like we are starting on a lifelong journey together."

Acknowledgements

Hopefully you enjoyed reading this novel. If you liked it, kind response and reviews in print and/or online media would be so appreciated. So, thank you for your time and effort. It means very much!

Some of you might wonder whether Emma is me and Ozzie is my husband – heavens, no! Also, there is no Ealingham-on-Ouse, though there are many wonderful little villages out in the British Fens that might match the description.

I was inspired by running into a travelers' camp and their obvious separation from the rest of the villages around, years ago. I had already read Mikey Walsh's autobiography *Gipsy Boy*. There are countless websites about the Romany and their difficulties of "fitting" into European societies. Here are a few that helped me:

https://www.theguardian.com/lifeandstyle/2011/feb/25/truth-about-gypsy-traveller-life-women,

https://travellermovement.org.uk/gypsy-roma-and-traveller-history-and-culture, and https://www.bbc.com/news/uk-15020118.

As to hunting and shooting in England, I found these websites very helpful: https://www.gunsonpegs.com/shooting/duck/uk/east-anglia/Suffolk and https://www.riflemagazine.com/275-rigby-highland-stalker.

The real Barb Tope won a character named for herself on my Facebook page. Some of her features are real, most of them are a figment of my imagination – I hope she likes it.

My thanks go to all my reader and author friends who have been supporting and encouraging me to keep writing, who have invited me to book events, and who keep asking me to read my work publicly.

Thank you, Ben Sclair, for letting me write for The Suburban Times (https://thesubtimes.com/) and share news about my books and book events there.

Special thanks to Marianne Bull, Larry "D.L." Fowler, Harriet Heyda, Roger and Kathy Johansen aka The Sock Peddlers, Denise Mielimonka, Karen Lodder Rockwell (https://germangirlinamerica.com/), Lenore Rogers, Angela Schofield (https://alltastesgerman.com/), Pamela Lenz Sommer (https://thegermanradio.com/), and Dorothy Wilhelm (https://itsnevertoolate.com/).

Above all, thank you, Donald. Your support for my writing and the events around my books is selfless and loving. Your help with detail in so many fields is priceless and enriches my work. Without your endless patience, I'd not be able to do what I'm doing.

Susanne Bacon was born in Stuttgart, Germany, has a double Master's degree in literature and linguistics, and works as an author, journalist, and columnist. She lives with her husband in the South Puget Sound region in Washington State. You can contact her at www.facebook.com/susannebaconauthor or visit her website https://susannebaconauthor.com/.

Bulletproof is Susanne's second Emma Wilde novel.

Made in the USA
Monee, IL
23 January 2023